Seduce

Felicity Heaton

LONDON VAMPIRES SERIES

Covet
Crave
Seduce
Enslave
Bewitch
Unleash

Find out more at: www.felicityheaton.com

CHAPTER 1

Sera's attention wasn't on the show.

While her sire sat beside her in the sumptuous red velvet seats of the dark stalls, her focus fixed on the erotic acts playing out on the stage of Vampirerotique, Sera's gaze was elsewhere, drawn to a man who had been on her mind since the first time she had set eyes on him over a year ago.

He stood to her right at the edge of the theatre near the front row, shadows clinging to him as though they too were drawn to his lethal beauty, his own gaze on the stage.

Not once did it stray from the performance—not even when she prayed under her breath every second that it would come to rest on her—and never did the intensity of it lessen.

His pale icy eyes scrutinised everything, watching closely, as though he was studying it so he could give a blow-by-blow description of it to someone after it had ended.

Perhaps he did.

He often disappeared as soon as the show reached its climax with the bloodletting, heading through the double doors that led backstage to an area she could only imagine.

Her sire, Elizabeth, had described it for her a few times but she had always been more interested in learning more about the enigma that was the vampire who ran the theatre.

Antoine.

His name was as exotic as his looks. The deadly combination of lush chocolate brown hair, those intense pale blue eyes and his lithe figure that just screamed he would look like a god naked, was too much for her. The more she saw him, the more she wanted him.

Regardless of the warnings that her sire often whispered in her ear.

"Perhaps I should arrange for a seat closer to him next time?" Elizabeth hissed across at her, amusement ringing in her tone.

Sera tore her eyes away from Antoine, ashamed that she wasn't watching the show that had cost her sire a pretty penny. Elizabeth had been getting her better seats with each performance and Sera knew that the closer they were to the stage and the action, the more expensive the tickets became.

Not only that, but she had paid for Sera's new outfit of a lacy deep green camisole top that matched her eyes and tight black jeans that showed off her legs to perfection, and the new highlights in her long blonde hair as well as the makeover they had both enjoyed this evening before attending the theatre.

She tried to watch the show, concentrated hard on maintaining her focus on the act playing out on the black stage but she couldn't take in any of it. Her head swam, unable to keep track of what was happening, focus diverted by the drop-dead-gorgeous man who stood barely twenty feet away from her. She gritted her teeth and frowned, forcing her eyes to follow the performers. It didn't help.

Seats closer to the stage just meant closer to Antoine, presenting her with a much better view of him. A view she didn't want to squander.

Her gaze drifted back to him as though he had his own gravity and she was powerless against its pull. He stood side on to her, his tailored black trousers and crisp charcoal shirt accentuating his figure, igniting her imagination.

It raced to picture him naked.

Long legs and powerful thighs. Firm buttocks with sexy dimples above them. A lean muscled back that followed the sensual curve of his spine and flowed into strong shoulders that would be a pleasure to study as he moved. And finally, a chiselled torso blessed with rope after rope of honed muscles down his stomach and a chest that would feel solid beneath her cheek and palm as he held her protectively in his embrace.

Elizabeth giggled, the sound so out of place during the intense erotic performance that the dark-haired man in front of them looked over his shoulder and frowned.

"You don't want to get involved with him. It wouldn't end well," Elizabeth said.

Sera wished that her sire had waited for the man to turn away before saying that. Now he was frowning at them both, dark eyebrows drawn tight above red eyes.

Elizabeth dismissively waved her hand, long scarlet nails catching the bright colourful lights that illuminated the stage. "I'm not talking about you. You'll miss one of the best bits."

The man's frown hardened but he turned back to the show. Elizabeth swept her wavy dark red hair over her shoulder and returned her attention to the performance too. Sera fidgeted on her seat when she caught a glimpse of the man on stage.

Victor.

Elizabeth had worked with him during her time at the London theatre.

He had been with Vampirerotique since a few years after it had opened a century ago and was their star performer. The large brunet male was currently pumping a woman in centre stage, his fangs enormous as he growled and fucked her side on to the audience so they could witness the whole act.

The petite brunette bent over in front of him was moaning with each deep plunge of his cock, her hands grasping her knees and breasts swinging in time with his powerful thrusts.

Two other men were pleasuring human females a short distance from him. The men sat on the red velvet gold-framed couches, one on each, flanking Victor where he stood close to the front of the black stage. The human females under the thrall of the other two vampires were facing the audience, kneeling astride the one who controlled them, bouncing on his cock and groaning as they palmed their breasts.

Sera looked away, cheeks burning.

Elizabeth leaned towards her. "Besides, he's as frigid as a nun and as cold as ice. In the fifty years that I worked for him, I never once saw him with a woman. The only person he loves is his messed up brother, and that's one relationship you don't want to interfere with."

Sera had heard the warnings so many times now that they were losing their effect. Every time Elizabeth brought her to the theatre to watch a performance, she reiterated the long list of reasons why Sera shouldn't want Antoine.

Unfortunately, those warnings only made her want him even more. According to Elizabeth, the gorgeous male vampire had been alone for God only knew how long. Sera wanted to be the woman to smash his armour and tear down his defences, and end his loneliness.

If he was lonely.

Her gaze slid back to Antoine. He stood rod straight, posture perfect, shoulders tipped back as he continued to study the performance. The first few times she had seen him, she hadn't thought to ask her sire about him.

She had thought he was just one of the crowd stretching his legs. When Elizabeth had noticed her staring, she had told her that he was one of the owners of the theatre, and an aristocrat vampire. That had explained the tilt of his chin and the air of pride he wore, and perhaps even the coldness that settled on his face at times when he was greeting the more important guests before the show started.

He was so distant, even looked miles away as he studied the show, lost in thoughts that she wanted to know.

Elizabeth nudged her and she looked back at the stage, trying to keep her eyes off Antoine. If she couldn't recount at least half of what had happened, Elizabeth would give her an earful on their way back to the city centre apartment they shared.

Things were heating up on stage. Victor had finished with his vampire female and was now toying with one of the humans, a young redhead with full breasts.

The blond male vampire that had been with the female on the couch was with them, kissing her as Victor stood behind her, palming her breasts and rubbing himself against her backside. The blond male looked into her eyes and she turned obediently in his arms, coming to face Victor.

She stared at him. Or beyond him.

Her glassy expression said that the male now behind her wasn't lessening any of his control just yet.

It felt so wrong to watch a woman under the power of a vampire, unable to do anything to disobey her temporary master, but she couldn't deny that it turned her on a little. The woman wouldn't know any discomfort or panic. She was so deep under that she was probably experiencing the purest hit of pleasure she had ever had. Exactly what she had signed on for.

Elizabeth had let Sera in on a secret.

Apparently, all of the humans who participated in the shows had agreed to the erotic acts in exchange for a rather handsome amount of money.

Elizabeth said it hadn't always been that way, but modern times called for a modern approach, and it was far easier not to kill them. The humans knew they would be participating in an on-stage orgy for an audience, and most of them had done such acts before, they just didn't know what they shared that stage with.

Vampires.

That meant they also didn't know they would be doing things under hypnosis.

Not that many of the humans required hypnosis to make them fully participate. The blond male vampire had lessened his control over the redheaded female human bent over in front of him, letting her desire rule her instead, and she was moaning and writhing against him, rubbing herself against his long hard cock.

Sera stared, cheeks heating, as he slowly inched his erection into her body and Victor stepped up in front of the woman. She reached for his rigid cock and closed her eyes as she wrapped her lips around his full length, swallowing him each time he thrust into her mouth.

The man behind her pumped her at the same pace, drawn out and deep, slow enough that the audience was twitching for more.

Sera stared at the blond male, imagining Antoine behind her like that, his face a picture of pleasure as he slid in and out with long deep strokes.

Her gaze shot back to the man of her fantasy and she found he was still staring at the stage with the usual detached look on his face, as though the sight of two men on one woman didn't arouse him in the slightest. She supposed that he had probably seen enough shows that he was immune to their effect now.

A few impatient growls erupted through the theatre and he flicked a glance over the audience and then went back to watching the show.

Sera had tried to talk to him once, when he had passed her by after the show had ended with the feeding and the crowd were leaving.

He had blanked her.

He hadn't even glanced her way. He had walked straight past her as though she didn't exist. She had spoken loudly enough that he must have heard her. It was after that moment that Elizabeth had started with the warnings, revealing only a tantalising amount of information about the powerful handsome aristocrat, just enough to make Sera want him even more.

Now, she craved his eyes on her, wanted to hear him speak and know his voice at last, and above all, she wanted to look up into his eyes and try to see past the barriers around his heart so she could understand him.

Was his distance from everyone just because he was an aristocrat, or was there more to it than that?

A shriek from the stage melted into a moan of pleasure and the smell of human blood spilled through the air, encompassing her.

Antoine visibly tensed, his arms flexing beneath his charcoal tailored shirt, as though he had clenched his fists. His pale eyes darkened, changed just as hers did to reveal her true nature. He turned away and she feared he would leave earlier than usual and her chance would slip by once again.

She tugged on Elizabeth's arm and her sire sighed, rose to her feet, briefly applauded and then started along the row with her trailing behind. Her legs bumped several vampires who were still trying to watch the final act, absorbing the scent and the thrill of bloodshed. She didn't care for it herself. More important matters needed her attention.

The men and women she passed snarled at her, baring their fangs in her direction and leaning to one side in an attempt to see past her. She muttered her apologies, trying to move quickly so they didn't attack her. Elizabeth made that impossible. She moved slowly and with grace in her long scarlet dress, her head held high and no apologies leaving her lips.

Her sire was old enough to stand against these vampires should they choose to attack but Sera wasn't. It would be years before she had the strength of her sire. They reached the last person and broke out onto the wide strip of red carpet that lined the edge of the theatre.

"Antoine," Elizabeth called and he paused and swung back to face her.

Sera's heart almost stopped when his deep crimson gaze briefly flickered to her before returning to her sire.

Her nerves rose as he strolled up the incline to meet Elizabeth and Sera slowed, the gap between her and Elizabeth growing larger by the second.

What was she doing?

It had taken months for her to convince her sire to do this for her and now that she had finally agreed, her nerve was going to fail? She wanted this man's eyes on her, wanted to be alone with him, and the only way to get what she wanted was to get a job at the theatre.

If she made it past the interview, then Antoine would have to meet with her.

Elizabeth had said that he spoke with each new performer to ensure they were suitable for the theatre.

Sera just had to get the interview out of the way and then she would have the chance she wanted.

Once they were alone in his office, she would take a shot at convincing Antoine that she was the woman for him. Whatever the outcome of that meeting was, she would quit her role as a performer. She didn't intend to perform at the theatre.

Hell, no.

She didn't have the right sort of personality for that. She wanted to blush whenever she chanced a glance at the black and red stage set and saw what the couples on it were doing. If it weren't for Antoine's presence in the theatre and her sire's insistence that they have a little fun, she would never come to such a place.

"Callum," a deep male voice called out, sharp with authority, and Sera stopped dead.

Sweet mercy, Antoine had a voice that could tame even the wildest of angels.

That voice was a drug.

It went straight into her heart and raced through her veins, the effect sweeter than any amount of blood.

Sera turned towards her sire and Antoine, only to see that he was walking away, leaving her sire with another dark-haired man.

He was handsome, full of smiles as he spoke to Elizabeth, far warmer and more amiable than Antoine was but nowhere near as alluring. Elizabeth signalled her to join them and she did, moving past the vampires now spilling out of the stalls and watching Antoine leave at the same time.

She'd had a chance to meet him and she had blown it.

If she had only kept up with her sire, she would have been close to him, maybe would have caught his attention this time and had his eyes on her at last.

"Is this her?" the vampire called Callum said and ran a glance over her.

Sera kept still, feeling as though she was for sale as he moved around her, his eyes on her body, inspecting and scrutinising every inch.

He came back to stand before her and looked at Elizabeth. "The summer season will end soon so we'll have time to train her before the winter one begins but we need someone with natural talent. Does she have what it takes?"

Sera opened her mouth to speak but Elizabeth beat her to it.

"Absolutely. She's my child, Cal. It's all in the blood." Elizabeth smiled broadly at him, red lips curving perfectly. Her deep brown eyes shone with warmth and she swept her dark red hair over her shoulders, exposing their bare curves. "You know I am one of your best ever performers."

Callum nodded and the longer lengths of his cropped black hair fell down over one emerald green eye. He frowned and raked it back, and then ran a hand around the nape of his neck, drawing Sera's eyes to a set of dark marks on it.

A bite mark.

It looked deep and fresh too, no more than a night or two old.

Did he have a lover?

He looked at her again and Sera's gaze leapt to his.

She swallowed the desire to confess that her sire was lying and she had no natural talent for the sort of thing that he was talking about. She smiled instead, trying to look every bit as seductive as her sire. Elizabeth had been Vampirerotique's star female performer until she had decided to quit her job and return to her family instead. They had met shortly after that, and Elizabeth had turned her into a vampire. That was thirty years ago now. It had taken Sera most of those years to become accustomed to life as a vampire.

"Come by tomorrow night when we're closed," Callum said. "Now, if you'll excuse me."

"Thank you," Sera said and he smiled at her, nodded, and then disappeared into the crowd.

Their excited chatter filled the theatre, the people passing her by discussing the show and the finale. Other elite vampires were still in their seats, enjoying the lingering scent of blood and sharing an intimate moment of their own with their partners. Sometimes the kissing that happened post-performance in the stalls was more erotic than what occurred on stage.

Sera dragged her gaze away from one couple near the front who were going at it with wild abandon. They looked as though they wouldn't make it out of the theatre before they succumbed to their desire and took things a step further.

She glanced out of the corner of her eye at Elizabeth. "Does Callum have a lover?"

"I thought you had set your sights on Antoine?" Elizabeth laughed when she blushed and then her expression darkened. "A wife... and I've heard rumours that she's a werewolf."

A werewolf? Sera had expected the owners of an erotic theatre to be quite liberal and wild, but marrying a werewolf? She definitely hadn't expected that one.

"You're serious?" She never could tell with her sire.

The woman enjoyed a joke more than was natural. Sera supposed that you needed to have an easygoing attitude when you chose to spend fifty years participating in an on-stage orgy with people you hardly knew.

Her stomach turned.

Thank the Devil she wouldn't have to do such a thing to get her chance to speak with Antoine. Just an interview that she would ace thanks to her sire's tuition and then she would be in his office, alone with him. Just the thought stirred heat in her veins.

Since her sire had agreed to help her, she had spent every night trying to figure out how to win Antoine.

It wasn't going to be easy. She knew that much.

She'd had lovers in her human life and even in her vampire one, but she had never pursued a man before, not as she intended to with Antoine.

Elizabeth had laughed when she had confessed that and had told her that she should probably start with easier prey and work her way up to someone like Antoine. That gave her the feeling that she was going to fail.

What sort of woman would he desire?

He ran an erotic theatre and watched the beautiful women performing on his stage without the barest hint of desire in his expression. If they couldn't arouse him, what hope did she have?

Maybe he wasn't interested in women who worked at his theatre. If that was the case, was she only shooting down what slim chance she had with him by interviewing for a position as a performer?

"I need a drink, and you look as though you could use one too." Elizabeth grasped her wrist and tugged her towards the exit at the back of the theatre. "Come along, my pupil. You have a lot to learn before tomorrow night if you're going to have a snowball's chance in Hell of impressing that man."

Sera trudged along behind her sire, weaving through the lingering crowd. Elizabeth's warnings rang in her ears, one louder than the rest.

She glanced up at the three storeys of elegant boxes that lined the theatre. The gold on the carvings decorating the curved cream low walls that edged the private boxes reflected the warm lights that illuminated the heavy red velvet curtain now closed across the stage. Matching curtains hung at the back of the boxes, some of them open now that the performance had ended. Many of the boxes were empty but beautifully dressed ladies and gentlemen still occupied the others.

She spotted Antoine amongst a group in one of the boxes on the first tier. He was smiling. She had never seen him smile. It looked forced to her.

Hollow.

Even among his own kind, he was still distant, his eyes devoid of emotion as he put on a grand performance of his own.

Sera wasn't going to overcome the challenge of winning Antoine's heart just by meeting the man.

First, she had to break through a barrier that was beginning to look impenetrable.

He was an aristocrat, and an old one at that. Although he looked barely a day over thirty-five, he was in fact over a thousand years old. His brother, Snow, was almost twice his age.

Sera was an elite.

To an aristocrat, she was some sort of filth they scraped off their shoes and nothing made that clearer than the theatres. The aristocrats sat in their boxes, looking down on the elite gathered in the stalls, separated and distant from those they saw as commoners and mongrels.

That disdain for her kind was the reason why Antoine looked so glacial whenever he had to greet the more important members of the elite, and why he had failed to hear her when she had tried to speak with him. He wanted nothing to do with the elite vampires outside the small circle that were part of the theatre.

He would certainly want nothing to do with her.

Not only was she an elite, but she was a turned human.

She was the bottom rung of the social ladder and he was the top.

The elite that he deemed worthy of a moment of his time, that he greeted with gritted teeth in order to maintain good relations with her kind, were all born as vampires into families that had turned humans within their ranks. None of them were turned humans themselves.

Even Elizabeth was born of a vampire father and turned mother.

If Sera wanted to shatter Antoine's armour, she would have to convince him to see beyond the fact that she was a turned human.

Elizabeth had taught her a few things, weapons that she hadn't held in her arsenal before, but she wasn't sure if she was brave enough to risk using them on Antoine.

Could she do what Elizabeth had said it would take to shatter his defences?

Could she really seduce such a powerful man?

Sera curled her fingers into tight fists and stared at him. He paused in the middle of saying something to the aristocrat vampires in the box with him, slowly turned towards her and then lowered his eyes. They locked on her.

He had felt her watching him.

Her heart beat harder, thumping against her chest as her blood heated, but she held his gaze across the theatre stalls, refusing to back down.

The next time she saw him, she would be alone with him.

And she would seduce him.

CHAPTER 2

Sera paced in front of the black stage in the empty theatre. She had arrived a full thirty minutes early for her appointment.

An appointment she hadn't realised she'd had.

Callum hadn't specified a time for her interview.

He had just said to come by whenever as the theatre was closed.

So she had.

The woman who had shown her into the theatre had been very kind. One of the staff based on her short black dress that revealed far too much leg and bosom.

Sera reminded herself that she couldn't really judge the woman by the clothes she wore. After all, it was her uniform and Sera herself was trying out for a position as some sort of on-stage whore.

What on Earth must the woman have thought of her?

Perhaps Sera should have asked to interview for a position as one of the staff. Cleaning seemed infinitely more appealing, and possible for her, than being a performer in the shows. Antoine still would have met with her so they could sign her employment contracts.

Was it too late to change her mind?

She continued her pacing, her eyes roaming over the deep red velvet curtain that closed off most of the stage, leaving only a strip of painted black boards around three metres deep exposed, and twirled her long blonde hair around her fingers. It was so quiet in the theatre that even her breathing sounded loud in her ears.

How much longer did she have to wait?

And why were they interviewing her in the theatre itself?

Elizabeth had said they would take her to one of the meeting rooms or the offices to interview her. That was what she had gone through to get her position at the theatre decades ago.

Sera shook her hands at her sides and blew out a sigh, trying to expel her nerves.

Maybe the offices weren't vacant tonight or they wanted to give her a tour before the interview began. That seemed plausible.

One of the sets of double doors at the back opened and a bright beam of light cut down the length of the dimly lit theatre to her. She shielded her sensitive eyes with her hand and squinted so she could make out if someone was there.

Her heart stopped.

The doors closed.

Antoine strode down the aisle, long legs carrying him easily at a brisk pace, as handsome as ever in his silver-grey tailored shirt that emphasised his build and clung just right to his muscles, hinting at how delicious his body would look if he were naked and stirring her imagination into a frenzy. His black tie, crisp black trousers and polished leather shoes perfected his image of a businessman but made him look decadent and alluring at the same time.

Behind him walked the immense male vampire that she knew from the performances.

Victor.

His normally thick dark hair was gone, shaved to his scalp to reveal thin scar lines in places, giving him a menacing air as he followed Antoine, dressed in a tight black t-shirt and jeans.

Were they just passing through?

Her heart started again at a pace.

Please, God, say they were just passing through.

Antoine shoved his fingers through his deep brown hair, the action screaming of irritation as much as his scent on her senses. He was annoyed about something.

Was he angry with Victor for some reason?

Sera moved aside, keeping her back to the stage so they could easily pass her and go about their business. She tried to keep her eyes downcast but they refused to do as she ordered and snuck to Antoine, meeting his icy gaze.

The warm lights from the stage lit his face, chasing the shadows away, and she had her first real glimpse of him. He was so handsome regardless of the darkness he emanated and the coldness in his eyes. He looked like an aristocrat, princely with his straight nose, defined jaw and perfect bone structure.

Did he resemble his brother, Snow?

She couldn't imagine the devastating effect the two together would have on the female aristocrats at social gatherings.

Her heart did a flip in her chest.

Antoine alone had a devastating effect on her. She could be strong, had taken to life as a vampire with surprising ease according to her sire, and had a flair for luring male prey that she still couldn't quite believe.

She wanted to be that confident, sexy, attractive woman around this man, but whenever she set eyes on him, her heart trembled like a timid thing in her throat, her palms turned clammy, and she wanted to bolt.

It was only the deep pounding need he stirred in her, the intense inferno of arousal that flooded her veins like liquid fire whenever she was near him, that kept her feet in place.

She wanted this man.

It went beyond natural desire, or at least what she had experienced in the past. No man had ever had such a startling effect on her. It was soul-deep, more than just a carnal longing. It was as though her very happiness depended on her being in this man's strong arms.

He stopped right in front of her.

"Sera, I presume?" he said and her bones melted at the sound of his deep voice pronouncing her name.

She nodded and held out her hand.

He raised a dark eyebrow in her direction and didn't take it.

She lowered it again, feeling like a fool for thinking he would touch her, a turned human, and for the first time since she could remember, her gaze didn't want anything to do with him. She stared at the red carpet beneath her feet.

What in God's name was she doing here?

This was all going to go horribly wrong.

She was going to end up getting her heart smashed by this man.

Confidence.

Elizabeth had pounded that one word into her head more than any other. Sera was beautiful, alluring, sexy, smart and funny, and more than that, she was warm and caring.

She was a confident woman. She was.

Sera clung to her sire's words about her, trying to believe in them. They ran around her mind and she felt their effect, felt the confidence begin to flow through her.

Sera managed to convince her eyes to shift up. They didn't make it to his face. They stuck on his tie. Shiny black paisley contrasted against the matt black of the rest of the tie. It was fascinating. Truly. That was the only reason she was looking at it and not resolutely into his eyes as she had planned.

He huffed.

"Well, let's get on with this. I have other matters that require my attention and the night is not growing any younger." He sat down in one of the front row seats.

Sera glanced at Victor, and then at Antoine.

This change required a whole rethink of her plan.

She had expected Callum to be the one interviewing her, not Antoine, and she still wasn't sure why Victor was present. Was he here because, in the absence of Callum, the elite vampire she had met last night and who Elizabeth had told her dealt with sourcing performers, Antoine needed someone more intimate with performers to help him?

Victor peeled off his tight black t-shirt to reveal the ropes of hard muscle that lined his stomach and the twin slabs of granite that formed his chest.

Sera's cheeks flushed.

Oh. Lord have mercy. Victor wasn't here to help with the interview.

This wasn't an interview at all.

It was an audition.

Her heart thundered. Her limbs shook.

Panic prickled down her spine.

"Is there a problem?" Antoine frowned, his annoyance turning his scent bitter.

She knew he could sense all of her feelings and smell her fear, and she tried to get a grip on her emotions, but they bombarded her.

Was there a problem? Was there ever.

She hadn't expected she would have to perform with someone and she definitely hadn't anticipated that such a performance would take place in front of the man who was her reason for doing this whole crazy thing in the first place.

"I thought it was going to be an interview. My sire said she had an interview with Callum." Her voice trembled.

Good God, could she sound any more weak and feeble?

Suck it up or this whole ridiculous affair was going to be over before it even started. Such a powerful man would want nothing to do with a weak female. She pulled in a deep breath and held it but it did nothing to calm her growing panic.

Antoine huffed again. "We might have done things that way eighty years ago, but we do things this way now. So, begin."

He waved towards the stage.

Victor obediently leapt up onto it.

Sera remained firmly rooted to the spot on the red carpet between the stage and Antoine where he sat in the middle of the front row, her gaze fixed on his.

The coldness in his pale blue eyes was fathomless but mixed in with it and his scent was increasing irritation. If she didn't do something soon, he was going to toss her out on her backside for wasting his time.

She could do this. She would take it slow and pretend that Victor was Antoine, and come up with a new plan while she was at it. If luck was with her, she could conceive something before things went too far.

Just how far was he expecting things to go?

Before she could ask, Victor's hands were under her arms and she was on the stage. Her knees almost gave out when he released her and she wobbled.

Antoine sighed again and raised the stakes with a pinch of the bridge of his elegant straight nose.

"Not wise to keep the boss waiting," Victor whispered into her ear, his cool breath tickling her neck, and she shivered.

He pressed the full length of his body against her back and her eyes widened as the hard bulge in the front of his black jeans pushed against her bottom.

Heavens.

She swallowed.

Trembled.

This was not happening.

Antoine couldn't possibly expect her to perform with this man. She had seen him on stage, witnessed the sort of debauchery he did with women, and the size of his thing.

He would break her.

What alternative was there?

Either she performed or she ran like a chicken and lost her chance. Antoine would never look at her again.

Hell, she would never be able to look at him again.

She had said that she would do whatever it took to make him belong to her and she couldn't back down now that another challenge had presented itself.

She had come here to seduce Antoine.

Seduce him she would.

Fear crawled through her, obliterating her momentary resolve and confidence.

She wasn't ready for this. He was going to laugh at her.

Antoine cast a critical eye over her and then waved towards Victor. She yelped when he settled his hands on her waist and nuzzled her neck.

"Come on, sweetness, play with daddy," Victor purred.

Gross.

It was hard to resist the urge to elbow him in the stomach and kick him in the shin.

"Your fifteen minutes just became ten, Sera. Am I wasting my time here?" Antoine said and she shook her head.

She could do this.

She broke away from Victor and turned to face him. He was handsome but she wasn't attracted to him.

How was she supposed to do anything with a man she didn't desire?

"I am very busy, Sera. *Start.*"

She jumped at the word and wished Antoine would stop using her name. Whenever he rolled it off his tongue in his exotic mixed accent, fire flashed through her body, heating her blood, and she wanted to close her eyes and do wicked things.

Maybe she needed him to say it more. Maybe if he kept saying it, she would find the courage to do what was necessary.

Ten minutes.

Even that sounded like a lifetime.

Her gaze flicked over Victor. He was already topless and the large bulge in his tight jeans confirmed that he was already hard.

Where was she supposed to start?

Removing his jeans seemed like a good place.

She stalked over to him, doing her best to look sultry and alluring despite the fact that her jeans and t-shirt combo wasn't the sexiest outfit in the world.

Victor didn't seem to care about her casual attire. His eyes were on the prize already, locked on her breasts. She raised her hand, drifting it upwards over her chest, luring his eyes to her face. Much better. She didn't like his eyes on her body.

Her gaze locked with his.

Victor smirked at her, so obviously assured in his charms and looks.

She wanted to roll her eyes and tell him that he wasn't her type, that when she looked at him, she was really imagining Antoine. She ran her fingers over the ridges of his torso, his skin cool beneath them, and tilted her head back and held his dark gaze as she undid his belt.

Sera stepped back and tugged it hard, pulling it through the loops of his black jeans in one fast motion. Too fast. The flamboyant rise of her arm as the end came free caused the belt to whip across Victor's chest, leaving a red streak on his skin.

He growled at her.

She curled up on instinct and leapt backwards, dropping the belt.

Antoine looked thoroughly unimpressed when she risked a glance in his direction.

She tried to claw things back by doing a sexy little shuffle across the stage, her mind racing to remember the moves that Elizabeth had shown her and all the things she had witnessed in this theatre.

On this very stage.

A stage she was now performing on even though she had promised herself it would never come to this.

Sera tackled Victor's jeans, popping the buttons while clumsily kissing the whip mark across his chest. She gasped when the final button gave and his rigid cock sprang free, already eager for her. Her heart bolted into action again, galloping so quickly that she felt dizzy.

She looked at anything but his erection, battling her nerves and panic again.

It was just sex. Sex on a stage. Sex on a stage in front of a man whom she really desired and whose opinion of her was probably rapidly sinking into seeing her as just another whore for his theatre.

What the hell was she thinking?

Sera squeaked when Victor pulled her blue baby-doll t-shirt over her head, catching her blonde hair and yanking it at the same time, and exposed her torso to the chilly air of the theatre.

Antoine sighed and stood.

It was over.

He was going to tell her thanks but no thanks and kick her out for wasting his time.

"Leave," he said and she grabbed her t-shirt off Victor and went to put it on. "Not you."

Sera froze, clutching the top to her chest.

Victor casually buttoned his jeans, shot her a smile, and then dropped down off the black stage. He sauntered towards the doors at the edge of the theatre, opened them and disappeared from view.

Sera remained paused on the stage, waiting for Antoine to throw her out.

"I am not looking for solo acts, but clearly this is your first time on stage. Do you feel you can perform now?"

Sera didn't know what to say.

He wasn't kicking her out?

She swallowed and faced him.

He was serious.

He had made Victor leave so she would feel more comfortable, and she did. Being on stage in front of him still felt wrong, but the thought of performing for him alone had a strange appeal. If she had ever wanted a chance to seduce him, they didn't come more perfect than this.

She could do this.

She could tease him with a slow reveal of her body to his eyes only, and from there it would only be a small step to other more wicked things. She was sure that once she was nude and bared for him that the feel of his gaze on her would give her the confidence to take things further and really perform.

And she was sure that performance would give her the chance to crack the armour around his heart.

What had looked like it was going to end in disaster was now looking as though it was a chance at victory.

A chance that she wouldn't squander.

Sera nodded and dropped her t-shirt onto the scuffed black wooden boards.

Antoine's gaze flickered down to her bra-clad breasts and then he sat back in his red velvet chair in the middle of the front row and stretched his long legs out.

His eyes held hers, cool blue and beautiful, fixed on her with such intensity that her cheeks heated with a blush.

He waved his hand.

"Perform for me then."

CHAPTER 3

Antoine couldn't believe that Callum had roped him into this and he had allowed it to happen.

When the black-haired elite vampire had walked into his office earlier this evening and announced that he would have to interview Elizabeth's child because Kristina had managed to get an appointment for her first ultrasound, Antoine had done his best to convince the elite vampire to get another appointment for her.

He had even offered to arrange it himself.

He knew some of the best vampire doctors that money could buy and all of them were discreet.

Callum had refused to hear a word about it. The elite vampire was irritatingly stubborn when it came to matters surrounding his offspring or the werewolf bearing it.

Not that Callum being here tonight would have made much difference. The male had been distracted from the moment he had met Kristina close to three months ago and that had only grown worse when he had discovered that she was pregnant.

On top of that, Callum still hadn't apologised for the whole fiasco that had severely damage the theatre's reputation. Talk of what had occurred that night, and that Callum's lover was a werewolf, had spread like wildfire through vampire society. Attendance was down but Antoine could smooth things over with the elite and the aristocrats given time.

He sighed and relaxed into the theatre seat, trying to get his mind off business and onto the woman on stage. It was impossible when his anger was riding him so mercilessly.

What Callum had done wasn't the reason he was so annoyed. It was what he had done. It haunted him. He should never have allowed the performance that night to start, let alone degenerate to the level that it had.

If Kristina had died, Callum would never have forgiven him.

Antoine knew what it was like to lose someone you loved with every drop of blood in your body and it wasn't something he wanted Callum or anyone to go through.

Dark memories stirred at the back of his mind and he forced his focus back to the woman as she stripped.

Sera.

She deserved his attention since she had made the effort to pull strings to get on his stage. It was a shame that she had none of the talent of her sire. She was too young, and too new as a vampire. Her looks were appealing though and that was the only reason he was allowing her to continue. Youthful with clear flawless skin, a rosy hue to her cheeks, and dark eyes.

He couldn't make out the colour.

She skimmed her hands up her curves, past her bra and up the sides of her head, pulling her long hair up and tangling her hands in it, her eyes closing in apparent ecstasy. Blonde hair was always good on the stage. The lights played well on it. Her figure was better than average, with sumptuous curves and her navy lacy bra cupping what looked to be good firm handful-sized breasts. She ran her fingers over the bra cups, as though she had sensed his sudden desire to know what her nipples were like. He imagined them small and dark, sweet plums made for sucking.

Antoine cleared his throat and brought his focus back to appraising her as a performer.

She had nice hips. Her waist flared out into them just right, an hourglass figure made for tempting men's imaginations and rousing a hunger to sweep hands over those dangerous curves.

She unzipped her blue jeans and turned away from him, granting him a tantalising flash of matching lace panties that stirred his interest. His control slipped again but he reined it back and ran a glance over her bottom. Small, pert. She swayed her hips and teased him by lowering her jeans and then raising them again.

Was she wearing a thong or normal panties?

French knickers.

The vision of her in them flashed across his mind and he found himself leaning forwards as she edged her jeans down, eager to see if luck would be with him and she was wearing his favourite lacy little shorts.

Antoine leaned back, shocked to find that she had lured him in completely without him realising.

What was he doing?

It had been centuries since that had happened.

He had watched the performances each night, unaffected by the act, uninterested.

They were actors.

Every one of them beneath him.

His name and that of his older brother were on the licence for the theatre because it brought in the aristocrats with their money, not because he was debauched enough to want to watch people engaging in sexual intercourse on a stage, although the final act always got his blood pounding, just as it did any vampire.

That wasn't a good thing.

That was dangerous.

And so was this female.

She shimmied out of her jeans, revealing his worst nightmare.

Lacy navy French knickers.

They clung to her bottom but rode up it as she bent forwards to free her feet from her jeans, flashing smooth peachy globes that caused an unsettling need to step up on stage and run his hands over them to feel their softness.

She kicked her jeans away and then turned towards him, her smile sultry and her dark eyes meeting his. An errant wavy strand of her blonde hair caressed her neck and drew his gaze there. His urge to leap up on stage increased.

He wanted to clear the hair away from the slender column of her throat, revealing it to his eyes.

He would step around her then, keeping his hand on her shoulder as he brushed his front across her back. His hard cock would nestle against her bottom as she arched into him, eager for harder contact between them, and he would lower his mouth to kiss the soft flawless skin and breathe her in.

He hungered to taste her and know her scent, to let it envelop him and send his desire soaring.

Antoine tamped down the need and pulled back on the reins again. He was in control here. This was all just an act designed to thrill. The desire in her eyes, the way she moved as though it was his eyes on her that made her want to do such a naughty little wriggle and put on a show were all fake.

Sera swayed her shoulders and then licked her lips and unhooked her bra. She let the lacy cups fall away from her breasts, revealing deep pink buds that made his blood cry out for him to give up his ridiculous need for control and get on stage with her.

That was not going to happen.

He glanced at his watch. More than ten minutes had passed. Part of him said to end it now, thank her for her time, and leave. It was safer that way.

Antoine looked back up to tell her just that but she stole his voice by running her hands over her bare breasts. Her hips rocked side to side, luring his gaze downwards, but he couldn't take his eyes off her hands. She teased her nipples between her fingers and thumbs, and Antoine realised that she was no longer nervous.

She stared straight at him, her eyes dark with desire that he could smell on her, bold in the way she held his gaze, as though daring him to come and see if he could make her feel better than she was already making herself.

Antoine forgot what he was supposed to be doing. He forgot the rules he had laid down, forgot everything that his family had hammered into his head about not interacting with elite beyond what was necessary, raising him to be a true aristocrat. He forgot it all.

What he didn't forget was how it had ended the last time he had let himself slip and fall, and how much he had despaired on discovering that she was gone, and how he had spent close to three centuries nursing the pain in his heart.

Antoine slammed the lid on his desire, stamping out the flickering spark of it in his chest.

Sera frowned as though she had seen the change in him, and then continued, and it seemed to Antoine that she had doubled her effort.

He felt dangerously close to slipping again.

She cupped her breasts and pinched her nipples, her gaze locked with his. He tried not to stare at her, fought it with every ounce of his will. When he managed to drag his eyes away, they betrayed him and fell to her hands, following them as she ran them over the flat plane of her stomach to her hips.

He stopped breathing when she slipped her fingers into her blue knickers and shifted her hips backwards, moaning as she touched herself.

Devil.

He bit back the growl that rolled up his throat and battled the hot rush of desire that came with it.

He wouldn't give in to her.

He wouldn't slip.

He was in control.

She moaned again, the sound filling the theatre and curling around him, taunting him. Her face was a picture of bliss, her eyes closed and rosy lips parted with satisfaction. He gripped the arms of the seat until his knuckles bleached and ached, refusing to fall for her act.

It wasn't going to happen.

Not now.

Not ever.

She was elite, a turned human no less. She was beneath him.

Devil, he wanted her beneath him.

Not going to happen.

His cock throbbed, telling him that it could easily happen. All he had to do was surrender the rigid control he insisted on having in his life, the ridiculous need for order and distance, and give in to his hunger.

He couldn't give in to his hunger.

The Devil only knew where that would lead him.

He knew exactly where, and the thought sobered him up so quickly it was as though someone had dumped a bucket of ice on his crotch.

Sera frowned again and Antoine knew she had seen the change this time. No doubt about it. She turned up the heat, trailing a finger up over her breasts, luring his gaze up with it, and then sucking it into her mouth.

He swallowed the dry lump in his throat and stared at her mouth, watching as she worked her tongue over the pale digit, twirling it around the tip. He throbbed in his black trousers again, aching at the beautifully erotic sight of her as she sucked one finger and touched herself with another.

His heart began to pound.

Nothing good would come of this.

He had to put an end to it now before it was too late.

He had to save himself.

"Shall I bring Victor back in?" His voice cut through the silence, loud in his ears. She stumbled, a blush heating her cheeks, and looked uncertain. "You are no use if you will not perform with a man... or a woman. I could have a woman brought in if that is your preference?"

The thought of her touching another man had his blood burning with rage. Touching a woman, however. That had a certain appeal.

Sera shook her head, grabbed her clothes, and headed for the steps down from the stage.

She was giving up?

That should have satisfied him.

So why did he want to block her exit and make her stay?

CHAPTER 4

"You aren't finished," Antoine said and Sera paused at the edge of the black stage, her clothes bundled in her arms.

Was his voice trembling?

Maybe it was just her hearing. She was shaking all over, partly due to desire and partly due to nerves.

He spoke again and his voice was tight, harsh. Hungry. "I want to see you finish... alone if you have to."

Sera risked a glance his way.

He stood a few feet below her.

Had he intended to stop her physically if she had tried to leave?

She couldn't believe that, or the spark of desire in his eyes. His enlarged pupils almost swallowed the whole of his pale blue irises. Sera ran her eyes over him and found confirmation that she wasn't imagining that hunger in his gaze or his voice.

The outline of his hard cock was unmistakable in his dark formal trousers.

She had come here to seduce him and she was so close that she could almost taste victory. He had said that he wanted to see her finish and he didn't care if she did it alone.

So alone she would finish.

She placed her clothes back down on the stage, aware of her partial nudity and his eyes on her.

Did he like what he saw?

The thought that he did boosted her courage and gave her confidence, but did nothing to rekindle the sputtering flame of her desire.

Antoine sat again, his ice-blue eyes on her and his large hands resting over the ends of the arms of his chair. He had clutched them when she had been performing for him, had held them so tightly that his knuckles had burned white. She had felt as though he was holding himself back, stopping himself from doing something.

What?

That one question had burned in her mind, driven her to keep teasing him, to keep pushing him to see why he felt the need to restrain himself.

Did he want to touch her too?

Sera slowly walked back to the centre of the stage, closed her eyes and ran her hands over her bare breasts, her nipples tingling as she imagined that it was his hands on her now, his strong cool palms cupping and kneading her. Her teeth sank into her lower lip and she loosed a breathy moan, unable to contain it as she continued her fantasy.

He had told her to finish.

She knew what that meant.

He wanted to watch her climax.

Just the thought of achieving an orgasm while he was watching her had her heart pounding erratically and gave her the strength to keep going.

Her head tilted back and she lowered one hand, skimming it over her stomach and then her hip, down to her knickers. His gaze followed, boring into her, heating her blood until she was burning for him. Pretending it was his hands on her wasn't enough.

She wanted to feel them on her for real, wanted him to come to stand behind her and toy with her breasts while she fingered herself.

She ached to feel the hard press of his cock against her bottom and the soft wetness of his mouth on her shoulder.

Sera groaned and it came out as a growl.

Or had it?

She flicked one eye open and found Antoine gripping the arms of his seat again, his whole body taut and coiled. He had growled. Oh. Sweet mercy. The thought that she had torn such a feral sound from him had her close to coming undone.

The only thing that stopped her was the cold edge that still lingered in his eyes.

She would break through that.

Sera hooked her fingers into the waist of her knickers and swayed her hips as she slowly eased them down her thighs and then off her feet.

Antoine watched her every move like a hawk and she was tempted to toss her underwear at him just so she could see his reaction.

She kicked it aside instead, afraid that such a move would shatter whatever spell she had cast on him, and slipped her fingers back into her plush petals. Another groan left her but Antoine didn't growl with her this time. She was close now, hot all over, near to bursting. She wanted Antoine's eyes on her when it happened, wanted to make sure that she had the whole of his attention.

He was watching her but that could easily change.

Darkness crossed his handsome face when she pulled her hands upwards, trailing them up her sides and over her breasts.

She felt wicked as he frowned, his gaze clearly expressing that he hadn't wanted her to stop touching herself. Her eyes dropped to his crotch and the hard bulge there.

She wanted to touch that.

She burned with the need to run her hands over him and feel his heat.

Did he burn for that too?

Would he turn her away if she stepped down from the stage and tried to touch him?

It was too much of a risk right now.

She had to work him up first, had to push him to the very edge, and then when he was close to falling, she would make her move.

Sera turned away from him and took a deep breath. It felt so wrong, so dirty, but so damned good as she bent over, exposing herself to him, and heard his low restrained growl.

She held her ankle with one hand, reached between her legs with her other, and gave herself over to the pleasure so she didn't think about what she was doing.

She moaned with the first brush of her fingers over her own clitoris and then swirled them around it, her breathing quickening and blood burning again. Her heart pounded against her chest and she closed her eyes. Another groan escaped her, louder this time, and she bit her lip.

It felt so good.

So very good.

Antoine's gaze burned into her, heightening her awareness of him and making everything else disappear. She touched herself, breathing hard and fast, enjoying the feel of her fingers and the tingles that shot through her with their every brush over her aroused nub. Her other hand clutched her ankle, fingertips pressing in, and her head spun.

She wanted more. Was so very close.

Just a little more.

She moaned and worked her hips, rubbing her fingers over her clitoris at the same time, unable to stop herself as her desire reached a crescendo.

So close.

Cold air shifted behind her and something thrust into her slick channel, plunging deep into her core.

Sera cried out her climax, body shuddering and clenching the hard rod buried inside her.

Her hand slipped from her ankle and she almost collapsed in a heap on the stage but a strong hand held her hip, keeping her upright. She breathed fast, head spinning, confused and lost in the haze of her orgasm.

What had happened?

She had never experienced something so explosive and wild, so blissful and satisfying.

The cause of the Earth-shattering climax that had come upon her slowly pumped her once and then withdrew, and she realised that it was Antoine's fingers.

Sera gathered herself and then straightened on shaky legs and turned to face him where he stood on the stage behind her. He looked at her, dispassionate and cold.

"There, you can perform with another, but still not enough to work the stage."

Sera couldn't believe what he had done. She trembled all over, still reeling from it and her climax.

Had she won her game of seduction?

The look in his eyes said no.

He wanted her to leave.

She had been realistic when speaking to her sire about Antoine. She had known that she stood a slim chance with him and had prepared herself for the inevitable rejection. She had been so fixed on her feelings being one sided and him showing no interest in her at all that she wasn't sure what to do now that he had.

There was one thing she did know though.

He wanted her and she would be a fool to give up on him now.

She wasn't going to leave, not when she was so close to convincing him to take a chance on her. She had got him on stage and got him to touch her. She knew that if she had just a little more time with him that she might be able to make him see that the desire zipping between them wasn't an act. It was real.

"I can perform," Sera said, mustering her confidence so he didn't hear the nerves in her voice. She smiled and tilted her head to one side, running her gaze over him. The hard bulge in his trousers hadn't gone anywhere. That was a start. "Just give me a second chance."

Antoine frowned, his cold eyes turning dark, as though he didn't like the thought of her having a second chance with Victor. She had to be imagining that.

"But I want to be able to select my partner." Those words leaving her lips caused his frown to harden.

"An unusual request. I may be inclined to allow it providing you will actually perform."

Boy would she.

Her smile widened. "I promise I will if I can choose who I perform with."

The darkness in his eyes deepened and red ringed his irises at the same time as a wave of anger rolled over her. Her smile held.

Did he know how jealous he looked?

She wanted to ask him but didn't want him to kick her out. He had no reason to be jealous but the sight of him feeling such an emotion sent her confidence up another notch and gave her the strength to continue.

"Has someone here caught your eye?" he said, little more than a thick growl, and she nodded. "Name them and I will see if the vampire or human is available."

Something in his eyes said the chosen performer would probably never even reach the stage. He would deal with them savagely for catching her eye.

Her confidence skyrocketed and she bravely faced him, nude and still shaking from the climax he had given her.

She ran her hand down his chest, feeling the hardness of it through his tailored silver-grey shirt and looked deep into his blue eyes.

"I name you."

CHAPTER 5

Antoine wasn't sure that he had heard Sera correctly. He stood on the stage, frowning down into her eyes that he now realised were the deepest most alluring shade of green he had ever seen, and tried to comprehend what was happening.

Sera wanted to perform with him, on his own stage, as her audition?

The voice deep in his heart said that this wasn't an audition.

This was a game of seduction.

Sera had been watching him for months now. At first, he hadn't known it was Sera. Many people looked at him during the course of a performance, but none stared with the intensity that she did.

When he had grown tired of being watched, he had located her out of the corner of his eye, surreptitious enough that she would never have noticed it. An elite. He had ignored her after that.

It was only in the course of the past few minutes that he had realised she was his voyeur, and how ironic that he had been the one watching her touching herself when that revelation had come over him.

"I do not perform." The hard ache in his trousers said to go along with it this one time but his heart warned to end this now, before history repeated.

The theatre was a business, and it was his life now. He had no room for romantic entanglements and no desire to get involved with a beautiful, attractive young elite vampire who'd had him on his feet and gasping to plunge something other than his fingers into her so he could feel her climax.

Antoine shook that desire away.

"No," he said again but it was weaker this time and he knew she had noticed when the look of disappointment in her forest green eyes briefly lifted.

She was targeting him for some infernal reason.

She had watched him and then devised some scheme to get into his theatre and meet him.

Had she even arranged for Callum to be away tonight, or was that fate intervening to bring them together sooner than she had anticipated?

He cursed under his breath. He would send Sera home to Elizabeth with a harsh warning ringing in her ears and a note for her sire telling her to stay the hell away from the theatre.

His jaw ticked as he clamped his molars together.

"No." Antoine backed off a step, angry now that he'd had time to realise the lengths she had gone to in order to ensnare him.

He should never have sent Victor away. It was clearly the chance that she had been hoping for. With Victor performing with her, Antoine would have been able to maintain his distance and view her with a critical eye as a performer.

He had made a terrible mistake.

Letting her perform alone, for his eyes only, had brought it onto a more intimate level. She had reeled him in and he had fallen for her ploy. It wasn't going to happen again.

He would end this farce and send her home right now. "I do not touch elite."

Her face fell, hurt emanating from her in tangible waves that awakened an emotion in him that was all too familiar. Guilt.

"Where was that rule a few minutes ago when you were touching an elite vampire rather intimately?" she countered and he commended her on having the courage to stand up to him.

"A momentary lapse in good sense." His words drew a dark glare from her.

Her lips compressed into a thin line and her jaw tensed. Hurt became anger, flowing over him, whispering of her desire to strike him. His guard went up automatically, fingers curling into fists in readiness to stop her should she attempt an attack.

He doubted that she would.

He had only stated a fact.

He had lost control for a brief moment and suddenly he had been on stage, staring down at her backside and his fingers as they plunged deep into her heat. Beautifully deep. His focus switched to his right hand, to the fingers that had plundered her. She had felt so good around him, warm and wet, body milking him. His cock twitched and hardened again.

It was not going to happen.

The quicker his body got that message the better.

33

His eyes shifted downwards and the reminder that she was stark naked and stood only a few feet from him was an unwelcome one. He was back to square one. So hard in his trousers that it hurt and he knew she would notice the way his cock tented the black material. Denying his desire for her seemed pointless when she could see the evidence of it for herself.

He could perform with her.

It would be so easy, and so damn sweet.

Who was he fooling?

If she bent over right now, he would have a difficult time convincing himself not to pull out his erection and thrust it deep into her welcoming body. He wanted to be inside her, sheathed to the hilt as his fingers had been. Pumping. Pounding. Finding release with her and hearing her scream his name as he brought her to climax again.

He couldn't do this. He didn't want it. It had hurt too much last time and he had learned his lesson. Love was a fickle bitch and, to avoid the suffering he had endured, he had vowed to avoid all interaction with women. That vow of celibacy had lasted close to three centuries. His rigid control over his desires and needs had held firm. It had stood up to countless advances from aristocrat females.

Why had it failed him now?

Sera blinked slowly, the fire in her green eyes still burning brightly, telling him that she wasn't going to give up. She was going to get her way whether he liked it or not.

He had to admire her spirit.

Most women gave up on him quickly, as soon as he spoke and said something that they didn't like to hear.

Sera had taken several verbal blows and was still standing, still holding her ground and refusing to surrender. She was beautiful. Like a goddess of war as she stood there unashamed of her nude state, her golden wavy hair curled around her tipped-back shoulders and her gaze defiant in the way it held his, silently challenging him to try to make her leave.

All she needed was a golden chariot and a spear and she would be a vision worthy of a painting.

He would definitely hang such a canvas in his office and would likely spend the entire night just staring at it, fascinated and mesmerised by her.

She stalked towards him, so confident now, the glint in her eyes telling him that she had seen his desire, his attraction, in his gaze and that she knew he couldn't hold out against her.

His defences were weak where she was concerned. Her green gaze dropped to his trousers and then she smiled into his eyes, her silent thoughts coming through loud and clear, as though she had projected them into his mind. S

he had noticed the hard-on that he was sporting and she was willing to make it go away, to satisfy his every whim and need. Devil, he wanted that. He wanted it with a ferocity that startled him.

Antoine backed off.

"I am not interested," he said but it sounded feeble even to him.

Victory flashed in his goddess's eyes.

"Is there room in your show for real seduction, Antoine?" she husked and the way she spoke his name rent the barricade that had kept the flames of his passion banked for so many centuries.

Sparks broke through, igniting his blood and threatening to turn his control to ash.

She bit the tip of her index finger, revealing the barest hint of fang, and his heart smashed against his chest. Fire consumed him then, the thought of her biting him and of biting her fanning it into an inferno that incinerated everything in its path.

Blood. Fangs. Two very bad things.

His claws extended and pressed into his palms, spilling the scent of his own blood. He wanted to taste it. His hands shook. He wanted to taste her.

No.

That he couldn't allow. Never. It was too dangerous.

"Is there room for a woman who could take a man and change his no to a yes?" Sera ran her hand down his chest, her eyes on his.

She had to see the danger in them, the red obliterating the blue, the warning to keep away from him or risk the consequences of his terrible hunger. It ran in his blood, tainting it, whispering words of sweet release to him, of feeding until he had quenched his thirst and then continuing.

Not that.

Anything but that.

He witnessed the perils of such feeding every night when his brother woke screaming and thrashing against his restraints.

That same addiction ran in Antoine's veins, a dark master waiting for the day it would reign over him and do the same terrible things to him as it did to Snow.

He was already past the age at which Snow had exhibited the first signs of bloodlust. If he didn't keep control, if he didn't deny his needs, it would be game over for him too. It would only take one little slip.

Who would look after Snow if he lost himself to bloodlust too?

"Antoine?" Sera backed away, a nervous edge to her voice now.

He closed his eyes and lowered his head, turning it away from her. The Devil, he was close to saying yes to her without any need for seduction but he couldn't.

Antoine rallied, pushing away the chilling thought of succumbing to bloodlust and her seduction, and said, "No."

He pivoted on his heel and stalked towards the stage door, intent on leaving her and heading for the sanctuary of his office. He would fix himself a glass of blood to quench his hunger and then close his eyes for a while and claw back control.

"Haven't I already seduced you to a degree?" she called after him and he stopped dead. True. "I got you onto the stage with me... I aroused you until you couldn't resist participating."

He couldn't deny that.

His fingers were still moist from touching her and he had been fighting the temptation to lick them clean the whole time he had been talking to her.

What was he doing?

How had she cracked the armour around his emotions so easily?

She didn't belong with him. He belonged with no one. It was safer that way.

Safer for both of them.

Antoine looked down at his hands.

Blood. It covered them, crimson dripping from his fingertips and splattered up the sleeves of his silver-grey shirt.

He breathed hard, fighting the panic and the memories. The fear. It swamped him, pushing down and breaking apart his defences, closing his throat and tightening his chest. It prickled over every inch of his skin and blazed in his heart.

Antoine shut his eyes and breathed slowly and deeply. In. Out. Inhale. Exhale. Just as he had practiced so many times. Focus on his breathing. Let everything else fade away. No fear. No pain. No death. Just him, living, breathing. Alive not dead.

Not bleeding out.

When he finally opened his eyes again, the blood on his hands was gone and Sera was standing between him and the stage door, looking at him strangely.

Concerned?

The spark of desire that had enlarged her pupils was gone, erased by her frown and a steady, penetrating look that made him feel as though she was reaching past the barrier right that moment, seeking to seize the truth about his past from his heart.

Antoine closed his eyes, turned away from her, and released one final soothing breath.

It would turn out to be yet another mistake, would end with her cleaving open his heart, but he couldn't bring himself to leave.

He wanted to stay. He *needed* to stay.

For the first time in three centuries, he needed to surrender a fraction of control so he could lose himself in this woman.

He needed to be with someone.

With her.

Everything about her said that she could satisfy his needs, that she would be everything that he wanted her to be—gentle, tender and warm. She could even fix his broken heart if he was brave enough to let her try, foolish enough to believe that the feelings she showed him in her eyes at times were real and not an act.

His heart whispered that he could still get out now before it was too late. He didn't have to put himself through this Hell again.

Antoine dropped down off the stage and sat in the seat he had occupied during Sera's show for him.

He couldn't leave. It was already too late. He had touched her, had fallen under her spell, and now he needed more than just a taste of her.

He needed all of her.

Sera stood there on the stage, looking uncertain now.

Had she expected him to make this easy on her?

He couldn't, not when part of his heart was screaming at him to flee, that he was in danger and needed to escape right now. The desire she stirred in him, the attraction he felt towards her, might have made him stay but he still fought those feelings on instinct and his heart would continue to fight her as she tried to seduce him. The self-preservation instinct ran deep after three centuries, impossible to overcome without a little convincing.

Sera still stood there. Was she waiting for him to say or do something?

She blinked, long dark lashes shuttering her beautiful green irises, and when she was looking at him again, her confidence was back. She had said she could seduce a man, could turn his no into a yes.

He wasn't going to prove an easy challenge.

The darker part of him said to take all that he could from her, satisfying his every need without becoming attached, and then make her leave.

She was willing. She could host his body and his need for blood, and he could continue for another three centuries without physical or emotional contact with a woman.

That thought turned his stomach.

What sort of man was he becoming? Had everything his family bred into him brought him to this point, a man devoid of emotion, willing to use an innocent woman's feelings against her and then discard her?

Or had this new dark side of him been birthed in the aftermath of that horrific night?

Antoine closed his eyes against the memory.

When he opened them again, Sera stood before him, still gloriously nude.

She leaned over so her wavy blonde hair fell forwards to conceal her breasts and settled one hand on the arm of his seat. The other came to rest against his chest.

His eyes closed with the first brush of her lips over his cheek and he exhaled slowly, losing himself in the soft caress and the smell of her. Sweet like almonds and honeysuckle.

It had been so long since a woman had been this close to him that he couldn't remember how any of them had smelt, but he was sure that none of them had smelt as exotic and enticing as Sera.

She kissed down to his jaw and then onto his neck, teasing him with brief sweeps of her mouth.

Antoine tipped his head back and stifled a groan.

Her hand moved over him, feather light as it fluttered across his chest and then up to his throat. She grazed her fingers over it and then buried them into his hair.

His groan escaped him this time, the feel of her nails against his scalp too good to contain.

She sighed, her breath skimming hotly over his throat, and continued to kiss and suck it, driving him wild with the desire to feel her teeth pressing into his flesh.

Sera kissed under his jaw, his chin, the other side of his throat. Another moan slipped free when she sat sideways on his lap and ran her other hand firmly up his arm, tracing his muscles through his shirt while she continued to work at his throat, maddening him.

She sucked and nibbled his right earlobe and he tensed, clawed at the seat arms and wanted to growl at her to make her kiss him. He needed to feel her mouth on his, cursed her for avoiding it as she kissed his cheek, his nose, and his chin. He tried to kiss her but she evaded him and clucked her tongue.

He was playing right into her hands.

A woman had done this to him before.

That instantly dampened his desire but it didn't kill it.

It rose from the ashes like a phoenix, reborn stronger than ever, given life by each brush of her hands over his chest and each sweep of her lips down his neck.

She tugged at his black tie, slid the two sides free of each other, and then started on his shirt. Her fingers teased his chest as she popped each button and slowly parted it.

Antoine couldn't take it.

He tensed right down to his soul, bracing himself as a desire to shove her away clawed at him. It was hard to deny that urge. He didn't want to be weak again, was afraid that if he gave in to her that he was only going to end up broken all over again.

His parents were right.

Never involve yourself with those below your class.

They had no breeding. They did as they pleased with no regard for others. Like animals.

Sera was one of those beasts.

That cooled his desire for a heartbeat of time.

What extinguished it completely were her fingers pausing against his chest and the sense of astonishment that flowed into him through them.

He was old and powerful enough to feel her emotions and he knew what she was looking at.

"My God," she whispered under her breath and touched one of the ridges of scar tissue that slashed across his chest. "What happened?"

Antoine didn't want to talk about it, and he didn't want to look down either. If he did, he wouldn't see her hand on his body. He would see something horrific. He would see his own flesh cleaved open, bleeding profusely, and his life draining before his eyes. He relived that nightmare often enough during sleep. He didn't need to see it while he was awake.

He grabbed her hand and shoved it off him, tugging his shirt closed at the same time.

"Nothing happened," he snarled and tried to push her away but she tensed, going so rigid that it was impossible to get her off his lap without sending her crashing onto the floor and hurting her.

Sera was still a moment, watching him in silence, and then she leaned towards him and did something that tore at the barrier he had carefully constructed around his heart.

She gently eased his hand away from his shirt, peeled it open to reveal his chest, and soothed each thick scar with soft warm kisses.

It was too much.

Antoine pushed the hand that grasped her wrist forwards, twisting it to an awkward position in an attempt to get her off him. She fought against him, still worshipping the scars of his past with kisses that eased his pain. It felt too good.

Each kiss punched another hole in his defences.

"You don't want to talk, that's fine," she murmured between kisses and he closed his eyes, his grip on her wrist tightening as he battled the temptation to wave a white flag and surrender to her.

For the first time, he found words lining up on his tongue, words that would reveal something terrible. Words he had promised he would never speak.

Who was this goddess on his lap?

What power did she have over him to make him so easily forget his pain and want to confide everything in her?

She licked the end of one ragged scar and leaned her cheek against his chest.

"You don't have to tell me anything, Antoine... but don't pretend you don't want me... or this." Her hand skated down over his stomach and his desire flared right back up when her soft palm cupped his hard cock through his black trousers. His breathing hitched and his jaw tensed, a hot flood of arousal sweeping through his veins and ratcheting his desire up to a whole new level. "This says you do."

Those four words were whispered against his chest and he couldn't deny the truth in them.

He did want her.

He didn't want this to end, whatever this was, even though he knew it would, whether he ended it before he got hurt or she ended it and hurt him.

"Let me taste you, Antoine. Stop fighting me." She pressed more soft kisses to his chest, her fingers toying with his nipples and then raking down his stomach towards his belt.

Where had this vixen come from?

She had been bold before, but this was different. He fixed his senses on her and could still feel her fear. She was scared, but not of him. She feared this wouldn't work and he wouldn't succumb to her advances. It wasn't because she wanted a job on his stage. It was because she wanted him.

Her desire wasn't an act.

It was real.

Just like his.

He closed his eyes when she undid his trousers, slipped her hand inside and drew his erect cock out. His breath hissed through his teeth and he tensed, her touch fire and bliss. He couldn't hold out against her much longer. His defences were dropping with each passing second and now he teetered on the edge of surrendering to her seduction.

It wasn't an act.

Just as he had lost awareness of their location, so had she. Her focus was so fixed on him and he thrilled at the feel of it, could sense her so clearly, and her pleasure. That alone intoxicated him as she shimmied off his lap to kneel before him and lowered her mouth, taking him into it.

He groaned, jaw clamped tightly and body taut, rigid with need.

Sera's warmth encompassed him, slick and wet, tongue expertly teasing him, tearing groan after moan from his throat.

Antoine gripped the arms of the seat and tipped his head right back, shallowly thrusting his hips as she sucked him.

Devil, it was game over.

His goddess had gone to war on his defences and was now assured of her victory. She was barely on him for ten seconds before he exploded in her mouth, unable to stop himself from climaxing. She moaned and he struggled to catch his breath, the riot of ecstasy rushing through him scattering his senses and making his mind swim.

It had been too long since he had found such a numbing release that he wasn't sure how to ease himself down from his high. He wasn't certain that he could even if he did know.

Before he could savour the bliss she had given him, cold awareness crept in at the corners of his mind, gaining ground with each rapid pound of his heart, until reality settled hard on him.

His sense of control snapped back into place.

Sera lifted her head and looked up into his eyes.

Antoine scowled down at her.

CHAPTER 6

Sera looked up at Antoine the moment she felt the change in him, sensed that the connection that had flared into life between them had been shut down in an instant. She could see it in his eyes too. The past hour with him had revealed something to her that she had never anticipated.

Antoine was a man with deep secrets, a man who didn't allow anyone to get close to him and who believed he had a good reason for remaining distant and alone.

She was a fool for not seeing it before.

Elizabeth had warned her about Antoine, but it seemed even her sire didn't know the man well or she would have mentioned that something terrible had happened to him, something he would never overcome.

Could never overcome.

The scars on his chest were shocking. It took a lot to kill an aristocrat, especially one as old as Antoine, but it looked as though someone had tried to put the limit of his healing ability to the test. Who had done such a terrible thing to him?

It wasn't only the scars on the outside that made him retain a sense of distance from everyone though. There were others on the inside, emotional scars that were as ragged and horrendous as the ones on his body as far as she could tell.

He was definitely a man with secrets, and he wasn't willing to share them with anyone.

Sera raised her hand, wanting to touch his face and tell him that whatever pain he had gone through, he could tell her about it. She would listen to him, never judging, only seeking to alleviate the burden on his heart so he no longer felt as though he had to walk through this world alone.

Antoine leaned back and warily eyed her hand, as though she sought to hurt rather than comfort him.

Game over.

She might have managed to make him surrender to his desire, but there was no way she could defeat the demons that held his heart captive. She didn't want a hollow affair with him. If she couldn't have all of him, she would rather have nothing at all.

Sera stood, walked to her clothes and slipped into her underwear. Her plan to dress completely before calmly taking her leave became impossible to fulfil when Antoine's icy gaze slid to her, tracking her every move. She grabbed the rest of her clothes, bundling them up in her arms, and flicked a dark glare his way before striding up the aisle towards one of the rear exits.

She made it halfway to the doors before turning around and storming back down to him.

"I just want to know why you shut me out again? Were you just out to use me or was this really just an audition?" Her voice hitched. It hurt to say that. She laughed bitterly at herself. "Forget it. I was stupid to think that someone like you could ever care about anyone but yourself. I've learned my lesson. Goodbye, Antoine."

Brave words.

She congratulated herself on them as she stalked towards the exits, swiftly now despite her trembling legs and the adrenaline pumping through her veins, determined to escape before her nerve failed. It was better this way.

Antoine would never give her what she wanted from him, what she needed, so there was no point in torturing herself by trying to win him over.

Sera was close to the doors, could almost taste her freedom, when she looked up to find Antoine blocking the exit ahead of her.

"Move," she said on a snarl.

He didn't.

She turned at the end of the rows of red velvet seats, aiming for the other exit further along the back wall of the theatre.

Antoine was there again before she could reach it.

He had moved faster than she had been able to see.

She stopped, a touch of fear in her blood now. She had heard that aristocrats, those of pure vampire blood, were more powerful than elites, and Antoine's age only added to the strength of his abilities.

He growled and stalked towards her, his eyebrows knitted into a scowl and darkness in his eyes.

No anger hit her senses but she wasn't going to hang around to ask what he was feeling behind his violent expression or place herself within striking distance.

Sera backed off, keeping pace with him. She bumped into the seats on one side of the aisle that led down into the stalls and threw a glance at the exit doors to her left.

Antoine was there again, stopping her mid-lunge, and forcing her down the aisle. She kept her eyes locked on him, her senses zeroed there too, and kept backing away.

Her attempt to flee hit an obstacle a short time later. Namely, the stage.

She pressed back against it, her senses sweeping the theatre, searching for another avenue of escape. The doors to her right and left were out of the question. Antoine would easily reach them before she could. Her strength couldn't compare with his, so fighting and subduing him wasn't going to happen either.

The only place that might offer her a chance of escape was the stage. She knew from the shows that there were doors to the left and right of it. They led backstage, which was a danger all in itself. God only knew who was back there, waiting in the wings. She had no desire to run into Victor again, not when she was only wearing her underwear.

"Sera," Antoine growled and she swallowed.

He shot towards her and she vaulted onto the stage. He slammed chest first into the wooden stage and unleashed a feral and vicious growl.

Sera dropped her clothes and went for the heavy red curtain that covered the rear half of the stage, intent on making it to the doors there.

Antoine tackled her just as she reached the velvet curtain, sending them both flying through it to the other side. She rolled painfully, legs tangling with his, and grunted when she hit something hard. One of the couches. Pain shot through her left shoulder and then she was on her back with both of her hands pinned above her head.

His cool breath washed over her face. "Why are you running from me, Sera?"

Why not?

The look of cold disdain that had been in his eyes was reason enough as far as she was concerned.

The fact that she had brought him to climax and he had shut her out the moment he had found release was another.

To top off those two, she added a third.

"You're scaring me."

Sera looked up at him, feeling the weight of his body against hers.

His open silver shirt draped over her and tickled her bare sides and his trousers were soft against her legs. He released one wrist and trailed his fingers over her cheek, and her eyes rose to meet his. Her fear of seeing the coldness in them melted under the warmth of his expression and the heat of the hunger in his blue eyes.

She didn't know how to react when he lowered his head and kissed her, hard and dominant, forcing her mouth open with his tongue. It tangled with hers, cool and teasing, luring her into submission.

She surrendered willingly, melting beneath him into the scuffed black stage, letting him lead as the kiss turned heated and passionate, a rough clashing of lips and teeth. Before she could think about what she was doing, she was raising her head off the stage, leaning into the kiss, seeking more from him.

Wasn't she supposed to be angry with him about something?

It popped back into her head.

He was obviously using her. He was never going to give her what she truly craved from him. He would seek shallow satisfaction from her, an emotionless sexual relationship, and she wouldn't be able to take it. She wasn't made for that sort of thing.

She couldn't.

The attraction she felt for him would blossom into something terrible, something that would end up killing her when he finally tired of her and cast her aside.

Sera slammed her fist into the side of his head, knocking him off her and into the red velvet couch beside them. She was on her feet before he could react, leaving him sitting on the floor.

"You are driving me crazy," he whispered, his eyes ringed by red and fixed on her.

He touched the bloom of crimson on his cheek where she had struck him and smiled grimly. At least it wasn't a forced smile. It was as real as they came, if not a little frightening.

What was he thinking in there? Did she drive him crazy in a good way, or a really bad way?

Was it wise to anger an aristocrat?

Antoine got to his feet, dusted down his black trousers, frowning at them, and then raised his head and looked straight back into her eyes.

At least the red had gone from his irises.

He raked his fingers through his thick dark brown hair. It was hard not to stare at the strip of body on view between the two sides of his open silver-grey shirt as he moved, his muscles flexing in a symphony so beautiful it would melt the hardest of hearts.

"Sera." He spoke her name on a sigh, a soft exhalation that made it sound like a prayer to God, a plea for salvation.

She would give it to him if he only asked it of her. She would share the burden that weighed him down. He only had to speak to her and let her in. He only had to give up his fight.

Sera stood her ground as he approached, his steps slow and cautious, as though he feared she would either lash out at him or bolt again should he move any faster. She probably would.

When he reached her, he brushed his knuckles across her cheek, curled his fingers around the nape of her neck, tangling them in her blonde hair, and lured her in for the softest kiss she had ever experienced.

It only lasted a bare second before he broke away to press his forehead to hers, their noses touching. He breathed hard, his chest brushing hers with each deep inhalation, and his fingers tightened against the nape of her neck, as though that brief kiss had been too much for him. It had been too much for her. The pleasure of it had been overwhelming, consuming, and devastating.

Her heart pounded, the beat as fast as the one in her mind. Antoine's.

"Sera," he whispered, supplicating her again, and she wished she knew what he wanted when he said her name that way so she could give it to him. He sighed. "I do not want to hurt you."

That was good. She didn't want that either. She could definitely go along with that.

He stroked her cheek with his other hand and pressed his forehead harder against hers.

His fingers clutched the back of her neck, his emotions taking a turn for the worse on her senses, so they blared in alarm.

Danger.

That wasn't good.

"Antoine?" she said, hoping to bring him back from whatever dark place his thoughts had taken him.

He growled. "I do not want to hurt you... but I do not want to end up hurt, either."

Sera reacted on instinct the second an immense wave of pain crashed over him and into her.

She wrapped her arms around his broad shoulders, pressing one hand against his shoulder blade and the other against the back of his head. He was surprisingly compliant, not fighting her as she moved and pulled him closer, so his head settled in the crook of her neck. His other arm snaked around her, fingers pressing in deeply, clutching her to him.

She frowned.

He was trembling.

What terrible scars did his heart bear?

She wanted to ask him that question but it would only drive him away.

He pressed a kiss to her shoulder, and then another, and worked towards her throat. She tipped her head to one side, letting him have his way, enjoying the softness of his mouth on her. He licked her, pressing his tongue into the line of her vein, and she moaned.

Questions burned in her mind, things she needed answers to and was sure would give her clues as to how to unlock his heart.

She wasn't brave enough to stop him and pose them. If she did, she would ruin the moment. He wouldn't answer them anyway. He wasn't a man who would do as others ordered. He did everything on his own terms. If he wanted to tell her, then he would, in his own time.

For now, she was satisfied with the knowledge that he didn't want to hurt her, and that part of his distance was because he too didn't want to be hurt by someone.

Again.

"Antoine." It was supposed to have come out as a question but it came out as a moan instead.

He nibbled her throat with blunt teeth, froze and swallowed hard, and then pulled aside to drop kisses on her bare shoulder instead. He hooked his fingers into the straps of her navy bra and pulled them down her arms.

Her hands moved to mimic him, pushing at his shirt so it fell away from his shoulders at the same time as he unhooked her bra and cast it aside. She tugged each sleeve off his arms and opened her eyes, intent on kissing her way across his shoulder and running her fingers over his muscled arms, and paused.

The scars continued on his arms, thick and pronounced, some of them so deep that they had pulled the muscle into a strange distorted shape. Sera went to touch one. Antoine growled and pulled away, scooped his shirt off the floor and put it back on, covering his body.

Shielding himself from her inquisitive eyes.

"Antoine," she whispered, as softly as she could, trying to show him that she hadn't intended to question him about the scars again and that he didn't need to hide them from her.

He turned his back on her and hung his head.

"Not quite what you thought I would look like?" he bit out on a dark snarl. "I bet you imagined me perfect, skin as flawless as your own, beautiful... not hideous."

That had her feet moving.

She came up behind him and slowly placed her hands on his shoulders so she didn't startle him. She swept her palms over them, feeling their strength, and then back again, to his neck. There, she slipped her hands into his collar and started to lower his silver-grey shirt again, revealing inch after inch of scars on his back.

He tensed.

Sera tiptoed and kissed each scar, from the ones that were barely a scratch to the ones that had damaged muscle irreparably. He didn't pull away. He remained motionless, rigid, his breathing shallow and controlled.

When her hands reached his, she tugged the cuffs of his shirt over them and then removed it completely. She tossed it away from them, onto one of the red velvet sofas that were part of the stage set, so he couldn't reach for it and hide from her again.

He began to relax as she continued to kiss and lick his skin, worshipping him, hoping to make him see that she thought he was beautiful, not hideous.

While she might have imagined flawless perfection as he had said, this revelation wasn't one that lessened the ferocity of her attraction to him.

Each scar was a story that she wanted to know, a memory that she wanted to hear so she could take away the pain he associated with it and could learn to love himself again.

She had been wrong about him.

He didn't love himself at all.

Sera slipped her arms under his and settled her hands on his chest at the same time as she rested her cheek against his strong back. She closed her eyes, her bare torso pressed against his cool skin, and held him in silence, hoping that he could feel every emotion that he stirred in her.

He was old and powerful enough to sense such things without skin contact.

With it, he should be able to read her clearly.

He should be able to feel that she still desired him, that she wished she could ease his pain and make him feel loved and beautiful. She ached for him.

Antoine shifted, his right hand settling over hers. She expected him to remove it from his chest but he held it there, pressed against him. He was taking the comfort she was offering. It was a start. Much better than the rejection she had anticipated at least.

She slipped her hands down from his chest to settle on his waist and began to kiss his back again, working her way around him and paying close attention to the deepest scar that had deformed the biceps and deltoid of his left arm.

When she reached the groove between the hard slabs of his pectorals, she rested her lips there, feeling his heart beating steadily against them. She breathed him in, liking the subtle fragrance of his strong blood that laced his cologne.

He drew in a deep breath. "Sera."

Sera lifted her head and met his ice-blue gaze. She had never seen it so soft, or him so vulnerable.

Was this what awaited her on the other side of his armour?

She was under no illusion that this brief glimpse of the other side would last longer than a few seconds. He was already fighting it, clawing back control over his emotions, seeking to distance himself.

Why couldn't he give in to what he wanted and take what he needed in order to heal at least his emotional pain?

She wouldn't let him close himself off again. Not before he had surrendered completely to his desire and found some relief, a few brief minutes away from whatever haunted his soul. She wanted to give him that at least. Even if it was all she could give him.

She tiptoed, intent on kissing him. He beat her to it, swooping down and claiming her mouth with his. She opened to him completely, letting him have his way with her, encouraging him with soft moans as he plundered her mouth with his tongue.

His hands clutched her bottom, dragging her against him, and she closed her eyes and surrendered to him.

She leaned into him as he lifted her, looping her arms around his neck and never breaking the kiss. His muscles flexed against her, sending a pleasant shiver tripping through her and deepening her desire.

She wanted to touch him all over, every inch of him, and put him to memory.

She wanted him to do the same to her, to caress and kiss her, to taste her and take her. She wanted to be his.

He settled her down on a red velvet chaise longue and covered her with his body.

The weight of him against her was delicious and she couldn't hold back the flood of desire that swept through her at the thought of him entering her, making love with her on the very set where erotic acts played out each night. She felt wicked and naughty, something she had never experienced before, and she liked it.

Antoine nuzzled her neck, devouring it with wet rough kisses, and leaned on one elbow above her. She moaned and arched into his hand as it covered her right breast, his thumb flicking over her nipple, teasing it to a hard peak. His answering groan against her throat was bliss.

He kissed downwards, palming her right breast as his mouth headed for her left. Sera wrapped her legs around his bare waist and buried her fingers in his thick brown hair, tangling it around them and clutching him to her.

The first touch of his tongue on her sensitive nipple caused her to arch into him again, her head tipping up to press into the soft cushioned back of the seat. Her lips parted with her moan, legs tightening around him as he sucked her nipple into his mouth and rolled it between his teeth, adding a bite of pain to her pleasure.

"Antoine," she breathed, lost to the world, a slave to the sensations he stirred in her.

She pushed her breasts up further, eager for more, desperate to encourage him to give it to her. He groaned again and bit harder, sending a spark of pain shooting outwards over her body. The wake of it carried intense pleasure and she found herself silently begging him to do it again.

He suckled instead, torturing her with the softness when she wanted it hard.

Before she could consider what she was doing, her hands had left his hair and she was raking her nails down his back.

Antoine growled and bucked against her, and rewarded her wickedness by clamping his teeth down hard on her nipple. Sera moaned so loudly that she was certain the whole theatre would have heard her.

Was it wrong that she wanted more?

Just as Antoine had teased her by being gentle in the aftermath of his first bite, she teased him, lightly running her hands over his back, feeling the soft shifting contours of his muscles and the harsh ridges of scar tissue. He growled again and squeezed her right nipple between his index finger and thumb.

The shiver that exploded outwards from the hard bud tore another moan from her throat and she raked her nails down Antoine's back again, clawing at him and driving him on. He didn't need to be gentle with her. She enjoyed the pain as much as he did, loved the dark edge it gave to what was playing out between them.

He rocked his hips against her and she mewled, unsatisfied and annoyed by the way her underwear and his trousers dampened the pleasure she gained from his hard movements. She wanted him naked.

Sera brought her hands down, pressed them against his chest, and pushed him upwards.

He paused, breathing hard, gaze following her hands as she skimmed them downwards, heading for his belt. He groaned as she undid it, tackled his trousers, and shoved them down over his bottom.

Heaven.

She skated her hands over his backside, the twin firm globes too delicious to ignore. The temptation to make him stand and strip so she could see him fully nude and gloriously hard was too fierce to deny.

She tried to push him off her but he tensed. Sera frowned and met his gaze.

There was pain in his eyes again.

He opened his mouth to speak and she covered it with her hand, afraid that he would say that he had changed his mind and that he wanted her to leave.

She had to have this moment with him.

She had come too far, risked too much, and wanted her reward.

More than that, she wanted him to have this moment with her, so he could find some relief from whatever pain lived in his heart.

Antoine took hold of her hand. Sera used all of her strength to keep it over his mouth but even that wasn't enough. He easily brought her hand away from it, as though she hadn't resisted him at all, and then released it. He stroked her cheek.

"Sera... this... I..."

Please don't say to leave. It ran through her head on repeat. His eyes darkened, the pain in them growing more intense, and she found herself lifting her hand to his face and mirroring him by caressing his cheek. He closed his eyes.

"I do not wish to stop." A hint of a smile tugged at the corner of his sensual mouth. "I can feel you. I need to warn you though... if we do this, I may not be able... I may hurt you."

Oh. She had liked the playful nips and wicked bites, but something told her that he wasn't talking about that sort of pain. He was talking about losing control, and he was far more powerful than she was. With his strength, he could easily injure her without much effort, and potentially without realising it until it was too late.

"Why?" She had to ask. He had to have a reason for believing he might lose control and be a little too rough with her.

The smile twitched on his lips again before dying completely. "I have not had sex in close to three centuries."

Dear God.

Three hundred years without sex?

She had lived thirty years as a vampire and had been with a few other vampires in that time.

Nothing serious.

Just casual flings that hadn't lasted.

Going years without any male companionship had been a test for her.

She craved physical and emotional contact with others. She couldn't even begin to imagine living three hundred years without being intimate with someone.

"Say something." It was spoken softly but there was a command laced into his tone, subtle enough that it could have easily gone unnoticed.

He wanted to hear her response to his confession and she was making him impatient.

"You've got a hell of a lot of lost pleasure to make up for," she said and was surprised at herself. Brash and bold. Something she had never been able to master before tonight. She curled her fingers around the thick length of his cock and smiled into his eyes as he opened them and stared down into hers, a beautifully startled edge to his expression. "So what are we waiting for?"

Antoine snarled and swooped on her mouth, crushing her lips with his.

Sera wriggled lower on the chaise longue beneath him, her hands shoving his trousers down to his knees at the same time. She moaned as he plundered her mouth, bruising in his force, so rough that her heart pounded with excitement.

Would she ever be able to get enough of this man? Could she ever feel so free and so bold with anyone else?

Something about him brought it out in her. His strength, his power, his beauty, and his past—all of it dark and enticing, driving her to embrace her own darker side. She clawed at his back, gasping between rough kisses, dizzy with passion and desire.

She raised her head off the padded seat, battling Antoine for dominance, nipping his lower lip and sucking it into her mouth.

The harder she sucked, the more frantic he became, until he tore away from her and forced his mouth on hers again, seizing control once more.

She let him take it, gave it over to him so she could focus elsewhere.

His cock.

He groaned when she tugged on it, sliding her hand up and down the long rigid length. She rubbed her thumb over the blunt head, smearing a pearl of moisture into the soft skin, and moaned at the thought of him filling her, thrusting into her and driving her wild.

Antoine seemed to read her mind.

He moved and before she could blink, she was face down on the chaise longue with him kneeling behind her. He grabbed her panties and pulled them down, yanking them off over her feet.

Sera wriggled, eager and excited, hungry for more.

He grasped her hips and pulled her up so she was kneeling before him and she thought he would give it to her, would give her the push she needed to tumble over the precipice and melt into bliss.

He moved over her instead, nestling his hard shaft against her, and kissed down her back. She moaned and closed her eyes, shifting her hands to the back of the chaise longue and holding onto it.

Antoine cupped her breasts, alternating between kneading them and tweaking her nipples as he continued to kiss her back and lazily rub himself against her.

"Antoine," she pleaded, wound too tight inside to take any more. She needed him inside her now. Wanted him.

"I want to kiss every inch of you," he murmured against her back.

"Later," she bit out in the midst of another moan and he chuckled.

She had never heard anything so beautiful.

Antoine had laughed.

Antoine *could* laugh.

She hadn't imagined it possible. She felt proud that she had made it happen but she still wasn't going to let him have his way. She wriggled her hips, rubbing herself up and down his cock, trying to coax him into entering her. Just the thought of that long thick length sliding into her had her close to coming undone.

"Antoine, please," she whispered and he groaned and lightly bit her back.

His hands left her breasts and he sat back, his body leaving hers completely. She felt bereft. Lost. She wanted him back, needed to feel him pressed against her, touching her.

He skimmed his hands over her bottom, moaning all the while, and she closed her eyes and joined him. His exploration was slow, torturous, and thrilling.

With her eyes closed, she couldn't see where he would go next.

Every sense she had heightened, focused on his hands, trying to predict their path. He eased them down, thumbs teasing the sides of her groin. One dipped in to brush her clitoris and she gasped, hips jerking upwards, hungry for another touch.

Antoine gave her what she wanted but it was more torturous than ever.

Rather than rubbing his thumb over her aroused nub, he used the head of his cock.

Her fingers tightened against the back of the chaise longue, arms trembling. She hung her head and moaned again, working her hips against him, desperate to encourage him higher.

He nudged her knees further apart and spread her with one hand. The head of his erection pressed into her slick core and he half moaned, half snarled, and then thrust his full length home.

Sera cried out, rocking forwards with the force of his entry, and shook all over.

He didn't give her a chance to recover her scattered senses. He grasped her hips and grunted as he withdrew and plunged into her again, hard and fast, setting a pace that had her pushing against the back of the chaise longue to hold herself steady. She hung her head again, breasts swinging, mind spinning.

Exquisite.

Antoine thrust deep into her, each one sending ripples of pleasure through her, tingles and shivers that all gathered into a swirling ball of heat in her abdomen.

That heat, that hunger, had her rocking backwards against him, forcing him to increase his pace, taking him as deeply as he could go.

She still wanted more.

Her fangs extended.

Her eyes changed, her irises melting to red at the same time as her pupils stretched and turned elliptical.

Sera looked over her shoulder, moaning in time with Antoine, needing to see him. His eyes met hers, feral and red, fangs enormous as he gritted his teeth and snarled. Just the sight of him and the thought that their coupling had unleashed his vampire side too had her plummeting over the edge. She cried out and shivered as she climaxed, body quivering around his thrusting cock and thighs trembling.

Antoine snarled again, hands clutching her hips, and adjusted his pace. His thrusts lengthened, drawing his hard cock almost all the way out of her before he plunged it back in, and she pushed through the haze of her first orgasm and found herself rocketing towards a second.

"Antoine," she moaned, needing to warn him that she would find a second release if he could only hold on.

"Sera." The sound of him uttering her name in such a pleasure-drenched voice had her close to begging him to say it again so she could hear his desire for her, his need.

He kept rocking deep into her, balls brushing her clitoris, sending sparks of heat straight to her stomach. She still needed more. She took one hand away from the back of the chaise longue and reached between her thighs. Antoine's hand left her hip, slid across her belly and covered hers. She groaned in time with him as they touched her together, his hand working hers.

"Come again for me, Sera," he growled and bent to kiss her back, nipping at it with sharp teeth.

The scent of blood tainted the air and she groaned at the blissful combination of his first suck on the cut, the feel of his hand guiding hers between her legs, and the deep slow thrust of his cock into her body.

It was too much.

Bright stars blinked across the velvet black of her screwed-shut eyes and she cried out, hoarse and loud, and jerked against Antoine as a white-hot wave of fire swept through her veins.

Antoine grunted against her back and slammed to a halt inside her, spilling his seed in deep throbs and pulses.

He moaned, breathing hard through his nose, still suckling the cut on her back. His fingers slowed their combined dance over her clitoris and she collapsed face first into the soft padded seat beneath her.

Antoine lay on top of her, his front pressed against her back, his body still intimately entwined with hers. He licked the small cut and rested his cheek against her back.

She could feel what he was going to say, so she answered his question before he could voice it.

"Damn... that felt good." Her fangs scraped her tongue as she spoke, a reminder that he had been better than that. Three centuries without sex clearly hadn't dampened his ability. She giggled, hazy and sated but still hungry for him. "More than good... I want to go again."

Antoine chuckled, the sound music to her ears. "Be careful what you wish for."

If he meant that he might fulfil that wish, then she would say it however many times it took for him to come good on that threat.

She quivered from head to toe.

Who would have thought that being rough could be so good?

Antoine pulled out of her and she continued to lay on the chaise longue, warm, fuzzy and content. It was only when she heard him moving around the stage that she opened her eyes.

He was dressing.

She frowned and tried to ignore the demon at the back of her mind that said he was going to kick her out now that he'd had his fun with her.

He gathered her clothes and she watched him as he picked out her knickers and her blue t-shirt. He knelt on the end of the seat by her feet and slipped her underwear over them and up her thighs. The brief caress of his fingers over the front of her pussy said that he wasn't going to kick her out just yet so she relaxed again. He ran his hands up her stomach, covered her breasts, and pulled her up onto her knees. His chest pressed against her back and he nibbled her shoulder before pulling away.

She let him put her t-shirt on for her and then waited while he retrieved the pile of her clothes. Rather than putting the rest on her, he slung them over his shoulder and then motioned for her to stand.

She did.

Antoine bent and scooped her up into his arms. She instinctively looped her arms around his neck.

"Where are we going?" Sera said as he carried her towards the stage exit.

"Somewhere more private." He raked his pale blue gaze over her, lingering longest on her bare legs. "I want to be alone with you."

Sera's eyes widened.

Meaning they hadn't been alone the whole time they had been together?

She looked beyond his broad shoulder and around the stage. There was no way someone could have watched them in here. The red velvet curtain was still down and the stage doors were closed. She would have heard if someone had opened them.

Had someone seen them together when they had been in the main area of the theatre?

Any number of people could have witnessed everything from the boxes that lined the sides of the theatre and she never would have known.

Sera blushed.

She really had put on a show, and not for Antoine.

They had both been the players in a private performance.

Heat flared in her veins.

She buried her head against Antoine's chest and let him carry her through a black walled room and up a set of stairs to the top floor of the theatre.

To a beautifully decorated black and gold corridor.

To his bedroom.

He set her down outside the mahogany panelled door, opened it for her to enter, and then closed it behind himself.

She stopped in the middle of his room and turned towards him, heart steady but her body fluttering at the thought of what might happen now.

Whatever happened, she was glad that it would be private this time.

She wasn't done with her seduction yet.

CHAPTER 7

Antoine remained with his back against his apartment door, his eyes on Sera as she padded around and snooped at his things.

What was he doing?

Things had almost gone too far back on the stage. He had come close to losing control. The taste of her blood had triggered thoughts of biting her and only his climax had subdued them. If he bit her, if he wrapped his lips around her open vein, he wouldn't be able to stop himself.

This was dangerous.

Yet he hadn't been able to let her leave after she had done her best to seduce him in the theatre seats. He knew he should have. It had been the most sensible course of action open to him. When she had given him a piece of her mind, hurt flashing through the anger in her eyes, and stormed away, he had meant to let her go.

Only he had ended up blocking her way and forcing her to stay.

She hadn't lied when she had confessed that he scared her. It was an easy emotion to sense in anyone, especially a vampire as young as she was. She had broadcasted it clearly. Half of the theatre would have noticed it.

Thankfully, their voyeur had left before that point.

They hadn't lingered long in the shadows of one of the boxes during Sera's attempted seduction. They had watched for barely a few seconds before leaving. They were strong too and he had a suspicion he knew who they were. Although they had masked their signature well, he was too familiar with them for them to fool him.

He could understand why they had come and checked on him. They had sensed his pain and wanted to protect him.

What would Sera say if she knew his own brother had witnessed her in all her naked glory?

She paused next to his bed and wrapped her hands around the carved black post nearest to him. Her smooth creamy legs were a luscious contrast against his deep red silk covers on his king-sized four-poster bed.

Would her beautiful blonde wavy hair look just as delicious splayed across his pillow as she slept in his arms?

He wanted to find out the answer to that question.

A foolish pursuit.

When he had confessed that he didn't want her to hurt him, she had looked as though she understood, had silently reassured him that she had no such intention. He hoped that had been the truth too, because now that he had tasted her, he wanted more, and he didn't want to let her go.

She felt too good, too right, in his arms. Her body fit perfectly against his, the taste of her kisses drove him crazy, and the satin of her caress made him wild. She was dangerous.

Addictive.

And wicked too.

There was innocence in her sometimes that contradicted the vixen she became when under the influence of her passion.

He liked the dual sides of her. The innocent and the vixen.

She was the innocent right now, leaning against his bedpost, watching him with wide wary green eyes and a blush on her cheeks. When she looked like that, he wanted to kiss her softly and make love with her, to be as gentle as a lamb so he didn't hurt such a precious bloom.

When she became the vixen, torturing him with claw and fang, he wanted to devour every inch of her and take her to her very limit of her wickedness and then send her careening over the edge into a dark bliss with him.

Which would she be now that they were alone?

Which did he want her to be?

He was all too aware that she fed off his behaviour. If he were gentle with her, she would remain that way. If he gave in to his darker urges, then she would too.

She cast her green gaze around his apartment, taking in the black walls, mahogany furniture, and the gilt-framed paintings. Her eyes lingered on them.

Did she like art?

He had quite the collection stored in the basement of the theatre in a secure, temperature and humidity controlled vault. In his bedroom, he preferred the works of the Italian masters. Original paintings by Da Vinci, Raphael, Botticelli and Caravaggio decorated his walls.

He had met some of them, fortunate enough to be alive during the wonderful renaissance period. He had been youthful then and carefree, full of the joys of the world and unaware of the dark times that lay ahead of him. The paintings were his link to those happier years of his life, granting him peace during his more troubled nights or days when images of the past haunted him.

He could lose himself in a single piece, mesmerised by the perfection of each brush stroke and touch of colour that brought the scene to life before his eyes.

"All yours I take it?" Sera said and he nodded.

She stepped forwards and leaned her back against the carved black bedpost, hands tucked behind her.

"Even those?" She jerked her chin towards the other corner of his bed.

Antoine frowned and looked there.

A set of thick steel and leather restraints hung with their short chain on the mattress and their cuffs dangling on either side of the bedpost.

"Those belong to my brother," he said and she looked relieved. "I keep a set on hand in case he needs them."

Her expression shifted, questions surfacing in her eyes that he would rather not answer so he turned away, walked to the chest of drawers that stood against the wall to the left of the door and poured himself a glass of blood.

He raised it to his lips and then lowered it again, set it down and fixed her a glass too.

Old habits died the hardest.

He wasn't used to drinking with company.

Definitely not in his room.

He never drank blood with his brother. Snow had a tendency to turn snappish and territorial when he fed, and was prone to lashing out at anyone who tried to come too close to his precious blood.

Would that be him one day?

Antoine picked up the two glasses and offered one to Sera.

She moved away from the bed, long legs luring his gaze to them and hips swaying just enough to catch his attention. He lifted his gaze back to hers when she took the glass and raised it in a salute.

She smiled.

Would she still smile at him when he was savage and unpredictable, lost deep in bloodlust that never relented?

Would she want to be with him then?

He still couldn't believe she wanted to be with him now. Or that he wanted to be with her.

When he looked at her now, he didn't see an elite, or a turned human. He saw a beautiful, strong woman who bravely stood up to him and refused to back down. She had seduced him, both his body and his heart.

His parents would turn in their grave.

He closed his eyes against the pain that welled up in his chest, choking him, and flinched as the glass in his hand shattered under the pressure of his grip, fragments cutting deep into his palm and fingers.

"God," Sera said and he wondered just how young she was that she retained some faith in such a power.

He mumbled a request to be excused under his breath and went through the door to his left, into the black-tiled bathroom.

Blood dripped from his hand and rolled down the sides of the obsidian oval sink.

Antoine picked the splinters of glass out, dropping them into the sink to swim amongst the blood, and ignored the scent as it filled his senses and tempted him to taste it. He flicked the gold tap around to cold and ran his hand under the water. The rush of it covered whatever Sera said to him and he glanced up at the mirror to see where she was.

The moment his eyes found her, the wave of her fear swept past him.

She stood in the bedroom with her side to him, staring at something.

Or someone.

Antoine turned and was in the room with her in under a second, standing between her and whoever had frightened her.

Snow.

His brother leaned in the open doorway, thick muscled arms folded across his broad bare chest, his icy blue eyes fixed on Sera. They flicked to Antoine as he came to a halt.

"You are hurt," Snow said, his voice a deep rasp that spoke of fatigue.

He had been disturbing his brother's rest far too often recently and the Devil only knew that Snow needed all the rest he could get. Battling his bloodlust drained his strength, giving the bastard demon that rode him a chance to overcome his control and send Snow into a feeding frenzy that only worsened his addiction.

Red ringed his brother's irises and his eyes tracked downwards, searching for the source of the scent of fresh blood now pervading the room.

The moment his eyes reached Antoine's hand, Snow growled and buried his fingers into his white overlong hair, clawing it back so hard that it pulled at his skin.

He screwed his face up, his agony palpable in Antoine's blood, fell to his knees with a harsh thud and curled over into a ball.

A deep shudder wracked Snow and he snarled. His back tensed and arms tautened, every sinew of his muscles visible beneath his skin.

Antoine rushed to his side and reached out to touch him, but Snow batted his hand away with such force that Antoine's arm snapped back and sharp pain buzzed along his bones. He realised his mistake. He had gone to touch him with his cut hand.

"Antoine?" Sera whispered, her fear colliding with his brother's agony, tearing him between them.

Antoine rushed into the bathroom, wrapped a small black towel around his hand, and then came back to Snow. Sera was in no immediate danger. He had to place his brother first.

"Snow." Antoine knelt beside him. His brother remained curled up, huge body rocking back and forth, his claws dug so deeply into his scalp that blood stained his white hair red in places. He touched his brother's wide muscled shoulder and felt it trembling. "Snow?"

Snow snarled, a tortured sound, one that Antoine had heard far too often.

"Sera." He didn't turn to look at her, couldn't take his focus off his brother.

There was no telling what Snow would do now that he had lost himself to the same horrific memories that haunted Antoine each day and was reliving them.

Or at least some of them.

Antoine was sure that others were buried so deeply in his brother's mind that he couldn't recall them at all.

"Yes?" Her voice shook, betraying her fear.

"The canister," he said and she moved an instant later, heading for the chest of drawers to his right and grabbing the blood.

She didn't hesitate to approach him, revealing the depth of her bravery. Most women he had met in his lifetime would have made a break for the door, or at least the safety of the bathroom. Not Sera. She had leapt into action, assisting him. Both kind and courageous.

She became more intoxicating with each new thing he learned about her.

Sera handed him the canister of blood and he knocked the cap off and lowered it under Snow's head.

Snow growled, pained and low, and turned his head to one side, trying to escape it.

Antoine persisted, knowing that his brother both needed and didn't need the blood. It would chase away the memories torturing him but would do so by replacing them with bloodlust, sending his brother into a mindless rage and hunger.

It was cruel but it was the only way Antoine could relieve his immediate suffering. When the bloodlust had him in its grip, he would forget everything but his craving.

Antoine risked moving the canister closer.

His brother snatched it, clawing him in the process, and was gone in a flash, retreated into the far corner of the room with his precious prize. He crouched there with his back against the corner, blood streaked white hair obscuring his face, radiating danger that warned Antoine to keep his distance or risk losing a limb or his life.

Antoine licked the cuts on the back of his hand and rose to his feet.

He reached out to Sera, placing his hand on her stomach and guiding her behind him, and eyed the cuffs hanging over the end of the bed and then the distance from them to his brother.

Almost equal.

If he made a lunge for them, there was a chance that Snow would realise his intent and reach them first.

Even if he did manage to grab them, he still had to get them on his brother.

Snow gulped the blood down, both strong hands locked around the fragile container, knuckles white from the force of his grip. Red rivulets spilled from the corners of his lips and trailed down his chin and neck.

Antoine needed more blood. Enough to keep Snow occupied long enough for Antoine to get the restraints on him without him noticing.

"Sera," Antoine said very slowly and quietly, trying not to draw Snow's attention to her. "Go into the bathroom and lock the door behind you."

"No."

It was such a determined response that he couldn't stop himself from looking at her and frowning.

"You can't handle this alone. You don't have to handle this alone." She stood resolutely behind him.

Dangerous words.

It was all too tempting to go along with her, to accept her help and accept that she was right in the process. He didn't have to handle this alone.

He could share this burden with her.

Something that wasn't going to happen.

Antoine shoved her so hard that she tripped across the floor and fell into the bathroom, ending up sprawled out rather indecently on the tiled floor. He moved faster than she could, shutting the door and holding it closed.

"Damn you, Antoine," she shouted through the solid mahogany.

Yes.

Damn him.

Damn him for wanting to protect her from his brother.

Damn him for needing to protect her full stop.

Snow lowered the canister, slowly opened his red eyes and looked up through the bloodstained ribbons of his white hair, fixing his attention on Antoine.

He growled and threw the empty vessel at him.

It shot towards Antoine with the force of a missile and at a speed that he barely managed to dodge and compacted against the wall, spraying remnants of blood across them.

Antoine knew what was coming.

He dived to his right just as Snow appeared before him and his brother careened into the wall. His impact shook the room. His snarl reverberated through Antoine.

Antoine rolled to his feet, skidded to the small refrigerator beside the chest of drawers and pulled the door open. He grabbed another canister of blood.

Snow inhaled deeply and purred.

That was not good.

Antoine's eyes flicked from his brother to the door right beside him.

Sera.

She had opened the door and was staring up into Snow's eyes, her own enormous. Her skin was the colour of moonlight, drained of blood as she stood only a few feet from Snow, within arm's reach.

Snow growled, lips peeling back from his enormous fangs.

That was not going to happen.

Antoine launched the canister of blood at Snow, hitting him square in the side of his head and knocking him backwards.

Snow roared.

Sera shrieked and shot back into the bathroom.

Antoine dived for the restraints.

He grabbed them, growling himself as the chain ended up between the corner of the mattress and the bedpost. He tugged and wriggled them, heart racing and head pounding.

Sera was still in danger.

Snow had the canister in one hand and was looking between it and the closed bathroom door, his face a picture of pensive darkness. He was trying to decide whether to tap the canister or Sera for blood.

"Snow," Antoine shouted, desperate to draw his attention away from Sera.

This wasn't going well.

He didn't want to harm his brother, had already been cruel to him by rousing his bloodlust, but he needed to take Snow down. He had to do it. He finally yanked the chain of the restraints free of his bed and then pulled the towel off his hand. He clenched his fist, causing blood to flow from the deep cuts.

Snow's eyes narrowed and his face twisted, distorting in pain once more.

Pain that wrenched at Antoine and caused tears to sting his eyes.

"No," Snow growled through gritted teeth. "It wasn't me. I didn't..."

He collapsed to his knees again, hitting the wooden floorboards with a spine-jolting crack. The canister spilled from his hand and he scrambled forwards, clumsily chasing it across the floor, his attempts to grab it sending it spinning and rolling towards the main door of the apartment.

"Javier!" Antoine yelled and smacked the restraints against the outside wall of his apartment, trying to get his neighbour's attention.

A little help wouldn't go amiss after all.

The elite vampire was in Antoine's apartment a heartbeat later, his deep brown eyes seeking the cause of his distress.

"Ay, Dios mio," Javier cursed softly in Spanish and then held his hand out to Antoine. Antoine tossed him one set of restraints and clutched the other. "How long has he been like this?"

"A few minutes. It is my fault. I cut myself and he came to check on me and smelt the blood. He's had half a canister and when he gets this one open, we will have a chance to capture him."

Javier nodded. It was a plan they both knew well and had successfully carried out countless times in the past.

"Antoine?" Sera's muffled voice coming from the bathroom seemed to throw Javier.

The Spaniard turned inquisitive eyes on him.

This was not the time for it.

Snow snarled and growled, sitting cross-legged on the floor in front of them, clawing at the metal canister. When he was like this, his brother was little more than a beast, unable to comprehend even something as simple as unscrewing a cap. His tension and frustration increased with each fumbled attempt.

When biting the metal container proved unsuccessful, Snow snarled at it, baring huge fangs in a threat, and turned his head this way and that, studying it for a weakness.

A true hunter.

It was going to end in a bloody mess as usual.

With a roar, Snow struck, puncturing the steel with his claws and shredding his fingers as he withdrew them. He didn't seem to notice his injuries. The victory he had gained over the canister and the sweet reward of blood overshadowed them.

Snow held the ravaged metal cylinder to his mouth, spilling more than he was drinking. It dripped down his bare torso as he rocked with the container, a deep rumbling purr emanating from him.

Javier nodded and they sprang into action.

Snow didn't even notice them. He was so focused on feeding that Antoine had his left hand cuffed and Javier had his right one secured without incident. Moving Snow would be a whole different matter.

When he realised he was restrained, he would fight them, and even with the help of the elite vampire, Antoine wouldn't be able to subdue his brother without taking a few knocks.

The bathroom door creaked open and Sera peeked out.

Antoine growled at Javier when he looked over his shoulder at her. If the Spaniard was looking at her bare legs, he was going to accidently-on-purpose hit him when Snow started misbehaving.

Snow perked up.

Lilah stood in the main doorway. She folded her arms across her chest, squashing her full breasts together in the small black tank she wore with her jeans. The tangled wet mess of her chestnut hair and the unimpressed look she tossed at both Antoine and Snow said that she had been showering with her mate, Javier, at the time of the disturbance.

Her golden eyes dropped back to Snow.

He purred.

She shook her head, calmly crossed the room to him, and ignored her mate's warning to stay away. She came to a crouch in front of Snow.

"I think that is quite enough, don't you?" She took the fractured bloody canister from him and set it down on the floor out of his reach.

Antoine tensed, waiting for his brother to explode and knock her aside, or worse, for taking away his favourite toy.

Snow lowered his head.

Ashamed? That was a new one.

Whatever dark power Lilah had over his brother, it was a gift given by the Devil himself. The woman was a witch when it came to Snow. No one could calm him as easily as she could.

Sera stepped out of the bathroom, a towel now wrapped around her waist to cover her partial nudity.

Snow looked towards her and tried to reach out to her but Javier's grip on his cuffed wrist was too firm. He whined and kept reaching for her. When Javier moved behind Snow and pulled on the chain so his elbow bent and his hand hit his shoulder, Snow tried with the one Antoine held, another low whine escaping him.

Perhaps it wasn't just Lilah who had power over Snow. Perhaps all females possessed an ability to soothe the beast of his bloodlust.

"He won't hurt you." Lilah smiled at Sera. "He's calm now. These two won't let you believe it, but it's true. See."

"Lilah!" Javier snapped but his mate was already laying her hand on Snow's bloodied cheek.

The large male vampire closed his eyes and leaned into the delicate hand on his face. He purred again, the deep rumbling sound filling the tense silence.

Lilah stroked his cheek and exhaled a long sigh, her golden eyes glittering with concern and tenderness.

It had been foolish of her to touch Snow when he was in such a strange mood.

She seemed oblivious to how dangerous his brother was, her faith that he was still Snow inside when the bloodlust seized him blinding her.

Antoine could only hope that Snow never proved her unwavering belief in him wrong. He would never forgive himself if Snow ever hurt her or any of the vampires he worked with at the theatre. He would feel responsible for his brother's actions because it had been his decision to conceal how dangerous Snow could become when the bloodlust took hold of him.

"Come along." Lilah rose to her feet and motioned for Snow to follow.

He lumbered onto his feet and obeyed her with only a few snarls and growls in Antoine and Javier's directions.

Antoine didn't want to leave Sera alone, not even for the few minutes it would take to cross the corridor to Snow's room and make sure that he was comfortable and secure, and had everything that he needed.

Lilah opened Snow's apartment door and held her hand out to Antoine, as though she had sensed his desire to return to his own room as quickly as possible.

"I think there's a woman in your apartment. I'm not going to ask what she's doing there, or mention how surprised I am, or how surprised Javier is too. I'm just going to say that I think we can handle things from here if you want to go back to her and make sure that she's okay. I promise that I will take good care of Snow." Lilah smiled broadly and as he set the chain into her hand, she added, "I will say that I think it's nice you have some company."

Antoine gritted his teeth and walked away, letting her have the last word.

He would never hear the end of it if he tried to argue that Sera wasn't going to be company in the way Lilah thought she was.

There were enough women distracting the owners of the theatre already, without him adding to the list.

CHAPTER 8

Antoine stepped back into his apartment and the relief he felt on seeing that Sera was unharmed overwhelmed him. Without thinking, he shut the door, crossed the room to her where she was cleaning the blood off the floorboards and pulled her up into his arms.

"You should have done as I said." The reprimand was supposed to come out strong and forceful, a scolding for her foolish actions.

It didn't.

It came out hoarse and in a whisper full of feelings that shocked him.

He hadn't felt his fear in the moment but it crashed over him now, only strengthened by the delay in his feeling it. His worst nightmare had almost come true.

If anything was going to give him the impetus to let Sera go before things became more intense between them, it was that.

He had tried to deny that any harm would befall her if he kept her, but he had been with her for barely an hour and already she had almost suffered the wrath of Snow's bloodlust.

"Antoine, you're shaking," she whispered and he realised that he was. "Come and sit down."

He was too tired to refuse and allowed her to lead him to the bed. Her hands grasped his shoulders and she forced him to sit on the edge of the king-sized mattress.

"Is your hand still bleeding?"

He didn't know.

He looked down at it.

Yes, it was.

The scratches on the back of his other hand were healing thanks to his saliva but he had left the wounds on his palm from the broken glass unattended.

She muttered something and knelt before him. He could only sit and stare as she took his hand in both of hers, palm upwards, and began to lick the cuts.

Heat chased away the cold numbness coursing through his veins. Awareness of each careful sweep of her tongue was only made more intense by the feelings that flowed from her into him as his blood in her body opened a deeper connection between them.

She was worried.

She wanted to take care of him.

She cared about him.

Antoine wasn't sure of the right reaction for that revelation.

Should he be happy that she had some sort of feelings for him?

It would have pleased him once, centuries ago. He would have easily fallen into her arms and passed blissful years with her, uncaring of where the future led them, living for the moment.

He wasn't that man anymore.

"Sera." He took his hand away from her and she looked up at him, her green eyes round and edged with the barest thread of crimson. The thoughts swimming in his mind hurt him. If they hurt him, they would surely wound her. "This cannot happen."

"Why?" she said, neither demanding nor yielding. Exactly the cool courage he had expected from her.

"Because."

She scoffed. "That is a lousy answer."

It was. He shrugged. What else was he supposed to say?

"You saw my brother." The way her face blanched confirmed that she had witnessed and understood the full horror of his brother's reaction and subsequent breakdown. "That same darkness flows in these veins."

He turned his palm back towards her, revealing the blood seeping from the cuts.

"My brother needs constant care. As constant as the bloodlust that seeks to rule him. My brother needs me."

"So, because your brother needs you, you don't get to be with anyone? You can't need anyone else, or have anyone else need you?"

He didn't really have a response to that one that she wouldn't be able to just bat aside and refuse to believe.

"Your brother relies on others. Your brother is not alone, detaching himself from the world. He has his demons, and he fights them, and he overcomes them... on his own. Restraining him didn't free him from whatever dark need had seized him. He freed himself when that woman came in. He was freeing himself when he was looking at me." Sera stood and sighed. "I could see it even if you couldn't. That woman was right. Snow wouldn't have hurt me."

"You cannot know that!" Antoine shot to his feet, his voice harsh in the quiet room.

Sera didn't back away.

She stood toe-to-toe with him.

Challenging him as always.

"What is it that you fear, Antoine?" she said coolly, holding his gaze and searching it, looking deep into his soul. There was no use trying to close it off to her. She had the key now and could unlock it at will. She had found her way past his defences. "Are you afraid that you'll lose control like that?"

"I am afraid I will kill you." He paced away from her and picked up the twisted remains of the two canisters.

He dumped them into the bin in the bathroom. The scent of blood followed him, strong and intoxicating. Antoine pressed his hands against the edge of the black counter surrounding the sink, ignoring the pain in his left hand, and drew in a deep breath.

Sera appeared in the doorway reflected in the mirror.

She sighed, stepped up behind him, and ran her hands over his shoulders.

Devil, just that simple motion of her hands felt too good for him to resist.

It told him to give up the fight and give in to her, seduced him into admitting that he liked the feel of her hands on him and the way it relaxed and comforted him. It had been too long since he had felt like this—cared about by someone other than Snow, close to someone and no longer alone in his quest to keep moving forward through his life.

The past centuries had felt like that, a constant march onwards, his focus solely on his brother so he didn't have to look too closely at himself.

Only Snow had kept him moving forward and it was all he could do to escape his past.

He refused to look back but now Sera had him balanced on the edge of doing just that, and surrendering to her demand to share his pain with her and embrace her and the fact that he didn't have to be alone if he didn't want to be.

He wasn't sure if he was strong enough to look back now without breaking down under the weight of it all.

It felt as though each year that had passed without him acknowledging what had happened had done nothing to lessen the pain he would feel if he allowed those memories to surface in his mind and his heart.

It felt as though each year had only increased it, and he was afraid that it would crush him now, would strip him of his strength and leave him broken. He didn't want to feel weak and vulnerable. Not again.

But the temptation to confess everything and share it with someone at last was strong, beating in his blood and his soul, coaxing him into putting voice to his past and letting it flow out of him in the hope that his pain would lessen by opening his heart to Sera.

Sera was strong, unyielding in her pursuit of him, but was she strong enough to handle his horrific past and the terrible future that awaited him?

"I'm not afraid, Antoine," she whispered as though she had read his thoughts and rested her cheek against his back, just as she had done on the stage before they had made love.

Antoine closed his eyes and absorbed the feel of her pressing against him, the intensity of the comfort it gave him, as though they were old lovers rather than practically strangers.

"You won't hurt me."

He wished he could believe that as fervently as she obviously did.

Antoine turned to pull her into his arms.

There was a knock at his door.

He sidestepped and passed her instead of surrendering to his need to hold her. Javier was at the door. The sandy-haired elite male smiled grimly at him, a smudge of blood on his cheek from where he had been struggling with Snow.

"Lilah has him settled now. She is singing a lullaby to him and says he will be sleeping by the end of it."

Antoine raised a single dark eyebrow.

Javier gave an easy shrug of his shoulders. "Don't ask me. Apparently, it works like a charm. He likes it when she reads to him too."

"I do not think it's wise for her to spend so much time around him, especially alone."

"You tell her that. I am her mate and her sire, and I cannot convince her to keep away from him. I can guarantee that if you visit him tomorrow night, you will see the difference it makes. He is often much calmer and more in control the night after Lilah has sung him to sleep."

Incredible.

His brother was not only a beast but a baby too.

The Devil, Antoine prayed he never succumbed to bloodlust.

He didn't want Sera singing him to sleep like a babe each morning just to have him sane the next night when he awoke.

Antoine paused.

How had she got under his skin so quickly? Hadn't he decided to end this?

Now he was thinking in terms of years down the line and he remembered all too well what had happened the last time he had started doing that.

Nothing but endless pain and misery.

A century of happiness gone in a heartbeat.

"Thank her for me," Antoine said and Javier looked as though he had just kneed him in the groin. His brown eyes were wide and his eyebrows were pinned high up his forehead.

Antoine huffed and closed the door in his face. Even he said thank you when someone had done something worthy of it.

"Antoine?" Sera's voice coming from his left rather than his right caused him to frown.

He turned and found her sitting on the edge of his bed, one bare leg bent at the knee and resting on the red silk covers, the ankle of it tucked under her other leg where it draped over the edge.

Temptation.

Which Sera was sitting before him now?

She must have snuck across the room whilst he had been talking to Javier and seated herself on his bed, so when he finished and turned away from the door he would find her there, beautifully arranged and waiting for him.

Challenging him.

The vixen.

The flash of wickedness in her green eyes gave her away.

It seemed his vixen wasn't going to heed any of his warnings. Stubborn minx.

Had Elizabeth warned her about him too?

He knew her sire well, and her sire knew him. There was no doubt in his mind that Elizabeth had recounted various reasons for her to snuff out her desire for him before it really got burning, but he found himself wanting to hear her admit it.

"You do not take warnings to heart, do you?" he said and she just shrugged and then leaned back on his bed, propping herself up on her hands.

She drew her foot out from under her thigh, dangling both of her legs over the edge of the bed and swinging them back and forth at opposite times.

Antoine stalked around her, keeping his distance, observing her and battling the temptation to surrender to her once again.

"No doubt Elizabeth told you not to involve yourself with me?"

She nodded. "Not so much involve. She told me not to even try. Said you were... as frigid as a nun and as cold as ice."

That one actually stung. Elizabeth had said that about him after everything he had done for her?

"Don't be angry with her. She doesn't seem to know you... the real you." Sera swung her legs forwards and propelled herself onto her feet. She stalked across the room towards him, hips swaying and her eyes on his, like a true predator. When she reached him, she trailed her fingers down his chest, her touch heating him to boiling point even with his silver-grey shirt dampening the feel of it. Sera tiptoed and brought her mouth to his ear. She whispered into it, "I know you now... I won't break, Antoine, and I won't hurt you... not unless you ask nicely."

Antoine growled.

It rumbled up his throat, a possessive hungry snarl. He wanted to deny what she had said, wanted to tell her that she was wrong and she didn't know him, and that he could so easily break her. He had seen the danger of the strength that flowed in his veins. Had witnessed it unleashed on those he loved.

And on himself.

The scars on his body burned, throbbing deeply, and he stepped backwards on instinct. Sera faltered, the confidence draining from her eyes. She thought he was distancing himself from her, that he was going to deny what she had said. He knew that he should.

He rubbed the scars on his chest through his shirt.

He couldn't bring himself to do it though.

Sera had offered him comfort and he was too weak to deny his need for it, and for her.

"What dark secrets do you have in your heart?" Sera slipped her hand over his and curled her fingers around so they pressed into his palm, stopping him from rubbing his chest. She drew their joined hands away and frowned. He did too. He had been smearing his own blood across his shirt and he had been so lost in his pain and the dark secrets she spoke of that he hadn't noticed. Sera sighed and pressed a kiss to the cuts on his palm. "You don't have to tell me. Not if you don't want to."

"I loved her for a century."

Sera went rigid, her lips frozen against his palm. It probably wasn't something a woman wanted to hear about but she had to suspect that another had hurt him, so it couldn't be unexpected. She should have been prepared to hear it. Maybe she had been, but she hadn't anticipated the length of the relationship he'd had with the woman who had broken his heart.

"She was an aristocrat," he said and Sera released his hand and turned her back on him.

"Oh." It was a small sound, one laced with defeat.

Antoine couldn't quite believe what he was going to say.

"I do not care that you are an elite, Sera."

Her shoulders tensed beneath her blue t-shirt. If she didn't believe him, she didn't say it. She turned towards him and blinked very slowly, her gaze assessing him. Searching for the truth.

"I mean it. Javier and Callum, even my brother, would probably pass out if they heard me say it... but I mean it. I thought it mattered. My family had always lectured me about the elite and our bloodline, and how we had to maintain the purity of it. I believed them once. But what good did it do us?"

His voice cracked on that last handful of words.

What good had it done them indeed?

If they had bred with humans and muddied their blood, they probably wouldn't have awoken the dark hunger that lay dormant in all members of their species. Years of selective breeding, of mating with only other aristocrat families, had kept their blood pure but the price for such purity had been a weakness none of them could have predicted.

His and Snow's generation were the first to experience bloodlust.

His family had paid dearly for their pride.

Very dearly.

Antoine slumped onto the bed and collapsed backwards onto the mattress, splaying his arms out across the cool crimson covers. He stared at the black canopy.

The bed depressed to his left and Sera's hand slipped under his. She was gentle as she inspected it and it touched him that she was still concerned about cuts that were nothing more than grazes compared with the open wounds on his heart.

"Anya was her name. We met and fell in love at a ball. One night of madness followed by a century of..."

"You don't have to go into details." Sera's grip on his hand tightened.

He flinched as his cuts reopened. Evidently, it wasn't wise to anger her by speaking of other women. She had asked to know his secrets. She would have to live with the truth of them.

"I loved her for a century and then three more."

"You love her even though she left you?" She dropped his hand.

He had deserved that. It had sounded as though he had just confessed his undying love for another woman.

"She left me without a word. I spent years, one hundred of them, looking for her at every ball and social gathering. I haunted the places we had stayed or visited frequently."

"Why did you stop searching for her if you love her so much?"

Antoine sighed and placed his hand on his chest. "Something happened that demanded my attention and deserved it more than a woman who had walked out on me."

"Your brother's bloodlust."

If only it were that simple.

"Snow had been suffering on and off with his bloodlust for many centuries. The symptoms had been minimal, inconsequential, so we thought it would remain that way. Doctors said that with regular, higher, intake of blood he would be fine." Antoine closed his eyes and cursed the name of those doctors for what felt like the millionth time. "I was so caught up in Anya that I just presumed Snow was doing well. I stopped checking on him and let him get on with his life. He never told me that the symptoms were getting worse and the attacks more frequent. I probably wouldn't have listened even if he had."

"You would have. It isn't your fault that he kept it secret from you."

"It is, Sera. I should have been there for him." He was sure that if he had been there for Snow, had continued to speak to him about his bloodlust and ensure that he was doing well that he could have averted the disaster that had befallen them. He should have been there for his beloved brother and it haunted him, filled his mind with images of how different things might have been.

"You can't spend your whole life focused on your brother's needs and his needs alone. He has a sickness, a disease, and that isn't your fault. You can't blame yourself for what happened."

"I didn't blame myself. I blamed my parents. I cursed my family for breeding this illness into us both. I knew that eventually I would walk the same dark path as my brother trod, and that, like him, I would be too proud to admit that the demon was seizing more and more control over me each night." Antoine sat up and dug his fingers through his brown hair. He stared into Sera's green eyes, the deep colour of them soothing away his agitation and coaxing him into continuing. Speaking to her felt so easy, as though she had come into this world for the sole purpose of hearing his woes and easing his pain. "When Anya left me, Snow found me drinking half the blood in the cold store and stopped me. He confessed that by drinking more blood, he had only quickened the awakening of his bloodlust and strengthened the hold it had on him."

"He wanted to save you from going through it too."

Antoine nodded. "So I owe him, not just for the warning that has helped me keep the bloodlust at bay for far longer than he was able... but because of what came after."

His throat closed, emotions squeezing it as memories bombarded him. He shut his eyes and frowned, struggling against them as they swept over him, crashing through his mind. Pain tore at his heart, until it felt as though it was going to kill him. He gritted his teeth and curled over. He couldn't do this. He had been wrong. He still couldn't talk about what had happened.

Sera frowned and cupped his cheek, her palm warm against his face. Her steady heart sounded in his ears, soothing and calming him, giving him something to focus on as he battled his pain.

She stroked his face, fingers soft against him, tender, conveying her concern. Her other arm settled across his back, hand curling around his shoulder. She leaned over and pressed a kiss to the shoulder closest to her and he wished he could feel her lips on his flesh, not his shirt.

"What happened?" Her hand fell from his face to his chest. He slowly opened his eyes and looked across at her. She stared down at her hand on his chest, her heart beating wildly now, as though she could see through his bloodstained shirt to his scarred flesh and was piecing things together for herself. "Did it have something to do with what happened to you? Did someone hurt you and make Snow lose control?"

Antoine laughed scornfully. "No."

He stood and paced across the room, needing the space.

"I was so busy looking for Anya that I didn't see the warning signs. Snow had confessed the depth of what he was going through. He had confided in me and I should have dropped everything so I could help him. Instead I was chasing after a ghost."

He reached out with his senses, across the corridor and into Snow's room. His brother was peaceful, at rest, and the depth of it surprised him. There was something in Lilah's lullabies after all.

"Snow had a bad night."

"How bad?" That question was cautious, wary, and conveyed that Sera knew just how badly he meant but she needed to hear him say it.

There was no way she could imagine the carnage he had witnessed.

Antoine turned towards her, weak from the grip that memories of that night had on his heart and his mind.

"A waking nightmare." Those two words fit the scenes playing out in his head so perfectly.

Sera reached out to him and he went to her, slipping his hand into hers and allowing her to lure him down to sit on the edge of the bed. She placed her arms around him and he didn't shirk her, just soaked up the comfort she offered and wondered what heavenly being had placed her on this Earth and brought her into his life. It felt as though she had been made for him.

"I have never told anyone this. Not even Snow knows the full story... although I suspect he remembers more than he admits."

She didn't tense. She started a slow motion of her hand over his back, stroking and soothing, calming his pain so he could speak.

Why did it feel so right to confide all of this in her? He had held it inside him for so long now. Everyone knew he and Snow had no other family but no one had ever questioned why. No one but he and his brother knew what had happened that night at their family mansion.

"What you saw tonight... that is Snow on a good day." He rested his head on her slender shoulder, seeking more comfort and warmth from her. He felt cold. He could still feel the icy blast of snow that had cut him to the bone that wintry night. He could still see the freshly fallen powder stained dark with blood. The place that had been such a core part of his life, full of happiness and security, love and warmth, had become a terrible vision of horror that had tainted his memories of his time there. Both his future and his past had been destroyed that night. "I came home late. It was barely a few hours before dawn. It was snowing heavily and the grounds seemed strangely quiet... the sort of quiet that sends the hairs on the back of your neck standing on their ends and triggers your senses to high alert."

"God, Antoine... Snow didn't—" She cut herself off, as though voicing her conclusion was too horrific, let alone hearing him confirm that it was right.

"There was no sign of the carnage from the front of the house but on entering it I found a bloodbath. My family, from my cousins' children to my aunts and uncles, all savaged to the point where I could no longer recognise any of them. I had thought it was hunters, but the attack was too brutal. Werewolves crossed my mind next. I heard a noise outside, coming from the back of the house. Every room I passed through to reach it was... I do not think I need to say." Antoine closed his eyes against the pain and focused on the soothing motion of Sera's hand across his back.

She was so warm and compassionate, taking away his hurt with her touch as though she was absorbing it into herself so he didn't have to suffer.

What strange magic had she worked on him to bring him to his knees so quickly?

It was too late now to turn back.

He would confess all, would confide these terrible things in her so she could witness the full brutality of his past and would know of what he too was capable.

"I found Snow trampling through the roses, drenched in blood, dragging our mother's corpse behind him. He was looking for something. I wasn't sure what it was until he turned and spotted me. Then I knew with chilling certainty that he was seeking more blood."

Sera stopped breathing, the motion of her hand against his back ceasing too.

She was still for too long. He needed to hear her speak, needed the reassurance that came with her steady caress.

He jumped and his heart lodged in his throat when she flung her arms around his shoulders and squeezed him tightly, her face buried in the crook of his neck. "My God, Antoine... your brother did those things to you."

Antoine tamped down the sharp wave of pain that threatened to tear through every scar on his body, unwilling to surrender to the past and afraid that the intensity of it would wake Snow. His brother needed his rest. He had vowed that night that he would do all in his power to ensure that Snow never suffered like that again, a slave to his bloodlust, mindlessly killing and unaware of what he was doing as he gorged himself.

"He did not mean to. It wasn't him who attacked me that night. It was the sickness that festers within him."

Sera tightened her hold on him. "He said something like that to you earlier. I heard him."

"He means it," Antoine said on a sigh. "I fought my brother and although he almost bested me, the familiar scent of the blood he was spilling and the sound of my voice eventually reached him. I brought him back but I didn't have the heart to do the right thing, not even when he begged."

"He wanted you to kill him." There was sorrow in her voice. He felt it in his blood too, but it was his sadness not hers.

"Was it cruel of me to refuse such a request? I forced him to promise me that he would never take his own life in payment for what he had done to me, and to our family. He was all that I had, and I love him. It was not Snow who wrought such horrific destruction that night. It was his bloodlust. I told him that, countless times. I promised him that together we would master it and he would be free again. I mean to keep that promise."

"You didn't want to be alone." Those words were whispered but each screamed in his ears as though she had shouted them.

There was a time once when he had convinced himself that he had refused Snow because he had wanted to help his brother and save his life.

That honourable intention had faded and worn over the years to reveal the uglier truth beneath.

He hadn't wanted to continue in this world alone, bearing the horror of what he had witnessed and what he had done. He hadn't wanted to kill his own flesh and blood, the brother who was everything to him, who he had looked up to all his life and loved more than anything in the world.

"I did not want to be alone," Antoine echoed, empty inside as the truth of it sank in. "So I made Snow suffer. I cannot lose him, Sera."

"I know." She pressed a kiss to his forehead and he sat back, wanting to look into her soothing forest green eyes and see in them that she didn't think he was despicable for the things he had done and she didn't fear the darkest part of him that would inevitably surface one day.

He needed to see that she knew what she was getting in to by choosing to be with him, before this went any further.

Sera smiled softly, her eyes full of understanding, overflowing with compassion and concern.

"You need to save him, not only because he is your brother and you love him, but because you need to know that you too can be saved."

Wise woman. She had seen through the mask of one intention to the others that lay hidden beneath.

"You are not your brother, Antoine." She stroked his cheek and then leaned in and pressed a soft kiss to his lips.

He wanted to drown in her then. Wanted to kiss her and make love with her in an attempt to lose himself and leave reality behind, forget everything they had talked about and the uncertainty of it all. Sera was good, and beautiful, and pure.

Perhaps as Lilah could sway Snow from the darkest moments of his bloodlust, Sera could protect him from the demon completely and help him hold it at bay so he never suffered as his brother had.

Perhaps.

"Are you part fae?" He searched her eyes, looking for something magical in them, a spark of fae power. It was possible for a fae to mate with a human. Her ancestors might have passed it through her bloodline to her.

She laughed. "I don't think so, why?"

Antoine brushed his fingers through the silken threads of her wavy ash blonde hair. "Whenever I look at you... whenever you touch me... I feel bewitched."

Sera smiled. "I think that's just plain old lust."

He shook his head. "No... it is deeper than that."

Her eyes widened.

His did too.

What he had said could be considered a sort of declaration, the kind that he had promised he would never make again.

It was the closest he could ever come to saying the words all women liked to hear, and it was far too early for those sorts of feelings between them.

"Maybe you've just been alone too long." Her smile became a wicked grin. "You need a woman's touch and some company, and that's all this has to be, Antoine, if that's all you can give me."

Antoine raked his gaze over her. She had to be part fae. A wicked sort of one. It would explain that aura of innocence she wore to mask her naughty side.

A side he wanted to become more acquainted with.

A side that was addictive.

She was willing to let this end.

He wasn't.

Now that he'd had a taste of her, not just her body but her warmth and the beauty of her nature, he wasn't willing to let her go.

Antoine placed his hands flat on the bed and kissed her, leaning forwards at the same time, driving her backwards until her head hit a deep red pillow.

She had sealed her fate by seducing him and there was no turning back, no matter what happened.

She was his now.

CHAPTER 9

Sera lay on the bed beside Antoine, watching him sleep.

The crimson silk bedclothes rode low on his hips, revealing a delicious muscular ridge that ran over his hip and downwards under the covers. Her gaze followed the deep brown curls back up to the sensual dip of his navel.

She wanted to lick that hollow.

Had a few times already.

Antoine laughed and told her to stop whenever she dipped her tongue into it.

It was hard to believe that the man lying next to her was the same one she had watched interacting coldly with others, keeping his distance.

He had changed so much since three nights ago when Snow had lost himself to a fit of bloodlust and Antoine had told her things that had left her feeling honoured, touched, and a little bit in love with him.

That he had never told anyone else the story of his past and what Snow had done, and had chosen to confide it all in her, still had her reeling to a degree.

He had lived through so much darkness and terror.

It made her want to give him light and love.

She gently brushed her fingertips across his brow and trailed them down the angular curves of his cheek to his jaw. He frowned and then sighed in his sleep. If he woke before midnight, it would surprise her. She felt worn out from their last bout of lovemaking, was tired to the bone and in need of sleep, but the sight of him kept her awake.

He frowned again.

Snarled.

His lips peeled back to reveal fangs.

Sera scooted backwards when he began to thrash side to side. He kicked at the covers, clawed at the pillows, and came close to hitting her.

"Antoine?" Sera got to her knees, nude in the middle of the bed.

He snarled again and lashed out.

She evaded his wild swings and grabbed his wrists, wrestling with him. The tighter she held him, the more he fought. He was too strong. Her heart pounded, eyes glued to his face as he growled. It was no longer fury in that thick snarl, but pain, endless agony that had her heart aching for him.

What horrible things was he reliving in his sleep? Was it the night that Snow had butchered their family and tried to kill him?

He kicked out, catching the bedpost with his foot and making the whole frame shudder.

"Antoine!" Sera pushed down on his wrists in an attempt to pin him to the mattress but it only made him struggle harder.

She didn't know what to do. Whatever he was dreaming about, he wanted to fight it and therefore he would fight her. He lashed out with his feet again, one tangling in the sheets and the other smashing hard into the black wooden bedpost.

He roared, his fangs enormous, and rolled his eyes.

Crimson irises flashed as brightly as coals.

Her blood chilled and sank to her toes.

The mahogany door burst open and she turned wide eyes on the intruder.

Snow's pale blue eyes were equally as large.

"Devil, female, cover yourself and release him. You are only doing more damage than good." He tossed the words at her on a dark commanding snarl and stalked into the room, the muscles of his broad bare torso shifting with each step, long legs tightly encased in black jeans.

Sera instantly grabbed the sheets, pulled them around herself, slipped off the bed and stood.

Snow rounded the foot of the bed to the side opposite her, furthest from the door, his bare feet silent on the wooden floorboards, his gaze on his brother were he lay naked on the mattress, still tossing and turning.

She kept her distance from Snow, torn between remaining near Antoine in case he needed her and maintaining a head start in case Snow turned violent.

Could she leave Antoine with him if he did?

No.

She knew the answer to that question without even needing to think about it.

She would protect Antoine no matter the risk. He had suffered enough for several lifetimes.

She couldn't let Snow hurt him.

She wouldn't let anyone hurt him.

"Is it bloodlust?" Those words trembled in the air between them for long seconds before Snow finally looked at her and shook his head.

"Just a nightmare, but not the sort I would recommend interrupting." Snow placed his hand on Antoine's forehead, his large palm and fingers easily spanning it. "Shh, Brother. All is well."

Amazingly, Antoine's movements began to calm, growing weaker with each second that Snow stroked his forehead. There was love in that touch, deep affection that showed on Snow's handsome face and shone in his icy eyes.

Snow's pale gaze shifted down to the scars on his brother's body and Sera caught the flicker of guilt that crossed his expression.

There was pain in it too.

Antoine had said that Snow didn't remember much about the night he had attacked him and killed the rest of their family, but he knew what he had done. Antoine struggled to cope with the things that had happened, the scars a constant reminder that he couldn't escape.

Those scars were not only a terrible reminder for Antoine but for Snow too.

How did he feel whenever he saw them, knowing that he had created them and had tried to kill his brother?

The pain crossing his expression as his gaze flickered over them was deep, fathomless, and he radiated clashing emotions of hatred and hurt. Sera felt sorry for him as she watched him struggling against his feelings. She couldn't imagine how terrible he felt, how responsible and guilty.

"He told me what happened." Although she whispered it, it came out sounding loud.

Snow didn't look at her.

His mouth quirked into a grim smile and his eyes roamed back to Antoine's face.

"Telling her our dark bedtime stories now are we? That isn't like you. She must be getting under your skin." Snow hunkered down close to Antoine and continued to caress his forehead.

Antoine's movements halted and his breathing turned heavy. Snow carefully lifted his left eyelid.

Pale beautiful blue irises.

Antoine had said she had some magic in her but Snow was the real fae here. He could soothe his brother even when he was sleeping, something she had failed to do.

"It would explain the nightmare." Snow frowned at Antoine and shifted his hand to his cheek, softly stroking it. It was strange to see such a lethal, dangerous man being so tender. It soothed her fear and left her feeling that she was seeing the other side of Snow, the man he was when the bloodlust wasn't riding him. She could understand the depth of Antoine's love for Snow now and why he desperately wanted to save him, because she could see the endless depth of Snow's love for him. "He hasn't told anyone before."

"I know." She still felt awed and honoured by that.

"He must like you." Snow smiled again but there was sorrow in it now and she recalled what Antoine had told her about him.

He had asked Antoine to kill him. It wasn't sorrow for his brother. It was sorrow for himself and the things he had done, and it was laced with an edge of finality and a sense of relief.

Snow still sought his death.

A permanent release from his suffering.

On top of that, he was watching his brother feel again, for a woman, and everyone in the room knew how well that had ended last time.

"He won't leave you," Sera said, afraid she was intruding and it would anger Snow, but unwilling to stand by and watch the man that Antoine loved so much believe that he was about to find himself alone again. "I swear to you, Snow. Your brother loves you and he feels guilty about his part in what happened to you and your family. He won't make the same mistake again. He would sooner leave me than leave you. He loves you."

"I know." Snow stood and towered over Antoine, immense and dark, lethal.

He seemed calm but he still radiated power, his formidable build only adding to the sense of danger he wore. She couldn't imagine how Antoine must have felt when he had battled his own brother and had almost lost.

She was surprised he had lasted in a fight at all.

Snow had killed their parents and others who were likely far older than he had been at the time. He had overpowered and murdered them all, but he had failed to kill his brother. Even in the darkest grip of his bloodlust, his love for his brother was stronger than his hunger for death and violence.

Snow huffed. "You do not have to fear me, female. Or for Antoine. I will not harm my brother."

"I have a name." Sera knelt on the bed, clutched the crimson sheets around her with one hand and shakily held the other out to him. He raised a pale eyebrow at it, as though the gesture was unfamiliar to him, or perhaps he just hadn't expected her to risk touching him and placing herself at his mercy. "Sera."

"Snow." He grasped her hand, his huge one engulfing hers, and the strength of his grip surprised her.

She had expected hard and tight, bone-crushing.

He was gentle and warm.

Antoine growled.

She looked down at him at the same time as Snow did.

"Hands off my female," Antoine snarled and launched his foot upwards.

It collided hard with their joined ones, knocking them apart and sending Sera crashing backwards. She managed to stop herself from falling off the bed completely and stepped down off the mattress. Her wrist throbbed, deep pulses spiked with sharp stabs, and she clutched it to her chest.

Antoine flipped onto his feet on the bed. Nude. Every muscle coiled in preparation.

"Antoine," she said and he turned towards her, red-ringed eyes losing their sharp edge as they met hers. She held her hand out to him. Just as Snow had turned docile in the presence of the newly-turned female vampire, Antoine's rage drained away and he blinked slowly. "I was just introducing myself."

"What were you doing in here in the first place?" Antoine turned back to Snow and casually stepped down off the bed, as though he hadn't just come close to unleashing a terrible violence on his brother.

He was an inch or two shorter than Snow, and of lighter build, but Sera knew without a doubt that he would fight his brother if he didn't like his answer.

"You had a nightmare," Sera said before Snow could utter a word, bringing Antoine's focus back to her.

It was probably safer that he hear things from her rather than his brother. If she could soothe his dormant darker side, then she had to be the one to explain. That way, Antoine wouldn't lose the cool that he seemed to have such a tentative grasp on.

She could see it in his eyes.

The red was gone but she had a feeling it still lingered, hidden behind those calm impassive irises that fixed on her, waiting to make itself known again.

She didn't want it to seize control of him.

She wouldn't let him suffer as his brother did.

"I didn't know what to do. You were fighting me. Snow came in and calmed you for me. That's all."

Antoine looked over his shoulder at Snow, and his brother nodded.

"Now, if you do not mind, I have seen enough of your bare arse for one night." Snow grinned and escorted himself to the door. He paused there and looked back at her. "Be gentle with him, Sera."

She rolled her eyes. She wasn't sure which Snow she preferred. The mindless demon or the sharp-tongued man intent on embarrassing both her and Antoine.

He closed the door behind him and her gaze crept back to Antoine.

Damn, did he look good stood there all naked and sleep ruffled, pale blue eyes possessively locked on her.

She shivered from the feel of them, awareness of him prickling across her skin and heating it, filling her with an intense need to cross the room to him, slide her hand around the nape of his neck, and kiss him. She wanted him again, couldn't get enough of him.

Would never get enough of him.

"I should go to work." He didn't move to hit the shower or get dressed.

He continued to stare at her, as though waiting for her to convince him to forget work, just as she had done each night since their first crazy one together.

He had taken a lot of convincing the second night and had put her powers of persuasion to the test. The third night he had taken less convincing. Right now, he looked as though he might be convincing himself.

"Do you often have nightmares?" Sera wanted to know what she was getting herself into so she could be prepared to deal with them.

Would running her fingers through his rich brown hair and speaking calmly to him, reassuring him, like Snow had work for her?

She hoped it would.

Antoine shrugged, the action causing his muscles to shift beautifully, luring her green gaze back down to his bare body. Her blood heated, desire scorching her veins until she was licking her lips and thinking about running her tongue over every delicious inch of him.

"More often than I probably remember. Sometimes I don't wake with Snow here, so I have no idea if I slept peacefully or not. Have I slept peacefully with you up until now?"

Sera nodded and a curl of her blonde hair fell down over her chest. Antoine's blue eyes followed it and burned into her, cranking her temperature up another notch.

She silently willed him to come to her and strip the red sheets away from her bare body, to run his hands over her and forget work and everything else and just spend another night lost in ecstasy with her.

"You've snored like a pig, but you've been relatively behaved before tonight."

He smiled and it was beautiful and full of warmth.

She had somehow cracked his armour and made it through to the other side to find herself face-to-face with a man more beautiful than she could have imagined.

She didn't care about the darkness he held within him, because she would help him conquer it, just as he helped his brother, sacrificing everything for him and never blaming him for the terrible things he had done.

How could she have ever thought that he was cold and unfeeling?

The things he had to deal with were enough to make anyone distant.

Antoine crossed the room to her, muscles moving in a breathtaking vision of masculine beauty, and raised his right hand to cup her cheek. He held it, his gaze locked on hers, so icy and cool, but full of heat.

"I did not hurt you?" he whispered and she shook her head. Her wrist had stopped throbbing now, her pain forgotten as she lost herself in watching him.

He looked her over, frowned at the silk sheets wrapped around her like a toga, and removed them just as she had desired. He dropped them on the bed and she closed her eyes as he inspected her, hands lingering in all the good places. His thumbs flicked over her nipples, teasing them into hard straining peaks, and then his hands skimmed over the curve of her waist and settled on her hips.

He moved around her and she bit her lip as he peppered her lower back with soft kisses, working his way upwards.

His hands skated over her stomach, pressing in and giving her a hint of his strength, and folded over her breasts, supporting them as he kissed her shoulders. "I do not want to hurt you."

"You won't."

He pressed his lips to her shoulder and sighed. "You do not know that."

"I do." Sera turned in his embrace, pressing the full length of her bare body against his solid muscled one. Delicious. "I trust you, Antoine. I trust that you won't hurt me, and I can prove it to you."

"How?"

"Wait here." She went to pass him but he grabbed her waist, curling his arm around and dragging her back against his front. She smiled over her shoulder at him and removed his hand from her. "I will be a whole two seconds. Trust me."

She grabbed one of his shirts off a pile near the door, slipped it on and did up a few of the buttons. It reached halfway down her thighs and smelt like Antoine, warm and spicy. He started to speak when she opened the door of his apartment but she didn't stop.

She crossed the black and gold hallway to his brother's door and knocked.

While Snow had a habit of just walking in unannounced, she would rather not.

Antoine had been angry enough when he had found her touching her brother in a gesture as innocent as a handshake. She didn't want to think about the scale of the fight that would erupt should she walk in on Snow when he was nude.

The door opened.

Snow raised an eyebrow at her.

She mirrored him.

It was a good thing she had knocked. The darkly beautiful man was wearing nothing more than the world's smallest towel around his hips and was dripping water all over his apartment floor.

"Can I borrow something?" Her heart flipped in her chest.

"Depends on what it is." He went to take a step back and then stopped. "I do not think it wise that you enter my room. My brother has claimed you as his female. I do not enjoy Javier's dark moods whenever Lilah enters my room without his consent. I have no desire to inflict such pain upon my brother. State what you desire and I will consider it."

Was Snow saying that he thought his brother was attached to her?

She had figured Antoine's outburst was just a momentary glitch brought about by his sleepy state.

She didn't dare hope that he was right. She had tried to keep her relationship with Antoine as physical as possible and not emotional, but the more time she spent with him, both intimately and afterwards when they would talk about his life and hers, the more she fell for him.

Her desire to make him see that they could be together was the reason she was here now, about to ask Snow for something that would likely embarrass him and Antoine as much as it did her.

"Those." She pointed, already blushing deeply and unable to say the words aloud.

Snow followed her finger, looking over his wide bare wet shoulders. His head snapped back around, white hair whipping with the force of the action, spraying droplets over her.

"The restraints?"

She cringed at the volume of those two words. Here she was trying to keep things subtle and he was shouting it at the top of his lungs.

"You want to tie my brother up?" He chuckled. "You are a dark little thing."

Her blush deepened.

It wasn't what he thought it was but she didn't correct him.

He lumbered across his room, leaving another trail of wet footprints on the wooden floor. He had the same taste in decor as Antoine.

Black, black and more black with the odd red accent.

His bed was something straight out of a torture chamber though.

The mattress looked comfortable enough, covered in black silk sheets and fluffed up pillows. The bed itself though. She had never seen anything like it.

Metal posts as thick as Snow's arms supported the four corners. The top and bottom of each post ended in wide square steel plates bolted to the ceiling and floor. On each bedpost, there was a length of inch-thick steel chain with an equally as thick cuff attached to the end. The leather lining the inside of the cuffs was cracked and stained dark with blood.

The bed looked as though it should have been strong enough to contain the most feral of creatures, but the posts were bent in places, dented and showing signs of wear.

"Seen enough?" Snow said and she jumped.

"I didn't mean to stare."

He shrugged casually but there was shame in his pale blue eyes. "I have my good nights and my bad nights."

So she had heard.

She glanced at the bed again, feeling sorry for him.

He had to chain himself to a bed, cage himself, whenever he had a bad night. Something told her that he used the restraints more often than that.

Did he sleep in them?

Chained and defenceless, open to attack?

One of the first things she had learned on becoming a vampire was how to protect herself by finding a secure place to sleep. While the general human population didn't know about vampires and the other creatures that shared their world with them, there were hunters out there who were constantly on the lookout for her kind.

"Snow," she said and he handed the restraints to her.

"Do not pity me," he snarled and closed the door in her face.

"He is right, Sera. It is his choice. I have always maintained that. Do not make him feel wretched for the choices he makes. He desires to protect others, those he cares about, and that is a noble thing."

Sera nodded and turned away from Snow's door, coming to face Antoine where he leaned against his doorframe a short distance along the corridor, wearing only his black boxer shorts.

He raised a dark eyebrow at the four sets of restraints in her hands. They were heavy, weighted with more than just steel and leather. What she was going to propose was dangerous, but she needed to show Antoine that she trusted him.

"Are those for me?" He nodded towards the cuffs.

Sera shook her head.

"They're for me."

His eyes widened.

She walked over and held the restraints out to him.

"I want you to use them on me. I will prove that I trust you and that you won't hurt me."

CHAPTER 10

"Sera." Antoine pushed away from the doorframe and Sera shook her head to silence him.

She knew what he would say. "I trust you, Antoine. You won't hurt me. I want to do this."

His pupils dilated, darkening his eyes with the heat of passion that said he wanted to do this too, but not because he wanted proof that she trusted him or that he wouldn't flip and hurt her. It was the thought of chaining her up that had him reaching out for the restraints, taking them from her, and leading her into his room.

He closed the door behind them and Sera exhaled slowly, trying to expel her rising nerves. She had never allowed anyone to restrain her before, not in her human life and certainly not in her vampire one. Just the thought of being chained, especially by industrial-strength restraints like the ones in Antoine's hands, handcuffs made for an ancient vampire, had her heart pounding and instincts kicking in.

They told her to flee, to end this before it began.

It was too dangerous.

She didn't care.

She had to make herself as vulnerable as she could be in order for Antoine to accept that she trusted him and that they could be together.

He needed to know that even when she was defenceless, open to attack and at his mercy, he could keep control and not let things go too far.

If she could show him that, he might believe that the bloodlust that silently lay in wait in his genes was something he could master and he didn't need to fear it.

Sera stripped off the borrowed shirt and set it down on the pile. Her gaze fell on the bundle of silk ties beside them and she lifted a black one, the material soft and sensuous against her fingers. Her heart flipped in her throat and her blood heated.

She bit her lip.

Mercy, she couldn't deny the fluttering desire in her belly that said she was already asking Antoine to cuff her, she might as well go all the way and ask him to blindfold her too.

When she turned to face him, the black silk tie dangling over her hand in front of her breasts, Antoine raised a dark eyebrow. He looked as though he was going to refuse the whole affair. Had she pushed too far?

He tossed the restraints onto the crumpled red sheets on his bed and crossed the room in a handful of swift strides.

She tensed as he snatched the tie from her fingers and stared at it, and then at her. She couldn't meet his gaze at first, was too busy watching the way his fingers shook against the tie.

He was nervous.

That made two of them.

"Turn around," he husked, voice thick with passion, roughened by desire.

Sera did as ordered, biting her lip the whole time. She tensed again when he stepped up behind her, his hips pressing against her bottom, and lowered his arms on either side of her head.

She couldn't take her eyes off the tie as he brought it towards her.

Her heart began to race, adrenaline mingling with the desire in her blood, a dangerous mix that Antoine ignited with a kiss. He worked his mouth along her shoulder towards her neck, teasing her as he secured the tie over her eyes, stealing away one of her senses.

Her instincts kicked in even stronger now, other senses on high alert. She could hear Antoine breathing and although it was shallow and soft, it sounded heavy and rough, filling her ears together with the sound of Snow pacing his room and Lilah's quiet giggle as Javier mumbled something in Spanish that sounded a lot like a curse.

Each brush of Antoine's lips over her shoulder drugged her, drove her deeper into her desire. The bare whispers of a kiss were the worst, sending glittering sparks over her skin and her senses into overdrive.

"Come with me," he murmured into her ear, his breath cool and teasing, melting her bones.

She already felt too hot, burning from just the brief kisses.

How would she feel when Antoine finally locked those heavy unbreakable cuffs around her wrists and ankles?

He led her to the bed, hands on her hips, guiding her through the darkness. She held her hands out in front of her, afraid of falling or hitting something. She trusted Antoine but she didn't trust herself. Without her sight to guide her, she feared she would make a fool of herself.

"Use your senses." Antoine paused with her, pressed a kiss to her shoulder and then lightly bit with blunt teeth.

She groaned.

How could he expect her to use her senses on anything other than him when he was doing such things to her?

The feel of his strong hands grasping her hips and his lips so close to her throat had every part of her locked onto him.

Sera expanded her senses to the room and her eyes widened behind the mask. Everything came back so clearly, outlined in her mind. Her memory of the room combined with the radar-like senses she had as a vampire gave her a clear image of where she was. She could have danced around the room blindfolded and not hit anything.

"Elizabeth needs to improve your lessons. Maybe I could teach you a few things. Would you like that?" Antoine kissed his way up her throat to her earlobe.

He teased it between his blunt teeth. His words evoked images in her mind of him playing the role of teacher while she pretended to be his naughty student.

Heavens.

Just the thought of acting out such wicked fantasies had her soaked with need and moaning for more.

Sera ground her bottom into his groin.

A sharp stab of pain in her earlobe caused her to flinch.

"Damn." Antoine was gone in a flash, leaving her alone and disorientated in the middle of the room.

Her senses reached for him and she was surprised to find him in the corner of the room.

"What's wrong?" She pushed the blindfold up her head and flinched again, the room too bright for her sensitive eyes even though the lights were low.

Red ringed Antoine's beautiful pale eyes.

Sera touched her earlobe and then stared at the trace of scarlet on her fingertips. Blood. She must have aroused him with her little grind against his crotch and brought his fangs out.

"Come kiss it better." Sera crooked her finger.

He shook his head and it dawned on her that when he said he was afraid of hurting her, this was what he meant. He didn't want to draw blood because doing so would push him towards the edge of an abyss, and falling into it meant succumbing to his bloodlust.

"You tasted my blood on the stage." She frowned, trying to figure out the rules he had set for himself when it came to blood.

"An accident. I shouldn't have. It was dangerous."

"You can control it when you only take a little though?"

He scrubbed a hand over his face. "Yes, but the temptation to draw more, Sera... I wanted to sink my fangs into you when we were together on the stage... I still want to now."

Sweet, sweet mercy, that sounded delicious.

She wanted that too but the pained edge to his eyes said not to ask it of him because he wouldn't give in to such a request.

He was protecting her.

Sera couldn't be angry with him for that. She didn't want to push him over the edge just to satisfy some personal itch to feel his fangs in her, taking her blood and opening a connection between them. The risk was too great.

The cut on her earlobe had already stopped bleeding thanks to her healing ability.

"What if I bit you?" she said and he groaned low and deeply, a feral hungry sound edged with pain, as though she was both arousing and tormenting him by suggesting such a thing. She wanted to know the boundaries so she couldn't accidentally cross them. "You're not the only one who gets an urge to bite when we're together."

"Sera," he groaned her name, hot and husky, sending a flash of fire through her blood.

She wanted to hear him say it that way as he kissed every inch of her, as he plunged his hard cock into her body and joined them as one.

"Can I bite you, Antoine?" Sera gathered her courage, overcame her nerves and ventured a step towards him. "I had a little taste too, remember? I want more."

"Sera." His eyes darkened, pupils eating up his irises. What remained of the blue gradually turned red and then the black circles of his pupils began to contract and lengthen, turning elliptical. His fangs emerged, pressing against his lips as he spoke. "I do not think I could keep control of my bloodlust if you did."

"It isn't bloodlust that makes you want to bite me, Antoine," she whispered and stepped up to him, tilting her head back to hold his crimson gaze as it bore into her, hungry and intent. "It's passion... desire. If it were bloodlust, you would want to bite me all the time."

"I do." Two dangerous words that came out rough and hard from between his teeth.

"No, you only want to bite me when you think about fucking me."

He growled and his hands shot to her waist, dragging her into his granite-hard body.

His mouth captured hers, rough and dominant, and she melted into him, loving just how possessive and fierce she made him.

She pushed her hands up his strong arms, delighting in the contours of his muscles that exuded power and filled her mind with images of him using it on her in bed, and tunnelled her fingers into the shorter hair at the back of his head.

He moaned with the first rake of her nails over his scalp and shuddered with the second.

Sera broke the kiss and moved her mouth to his neck before he could capture her lips again. She pressed her tongue into the vein and Antoine clutched her, pulling her hard against him, his fingertips sharp painful points against her hips.

"Don't," he whispered and he might have sounded more convincing had his right hand not left her waist and tangled into her blonde hair, pinning her mouth to his throat.

He wanted this as much as she did. There was nothing more sacred to a vampire than blood, and giving it to or taking it from another vampire was one of the most erotic, profound experiences they could have.

Sera's fangs extended and she gave his neck one more swift lick so he had time to prepare himself and then sank them deep into him.

Antoine growled, the feral noise carrying an intoxicating cocktail of desire, bliss, hunger and danger.

She released his neck, covered the twin puncture wounds with her mouth and sucked.

Antoine shivered and moaned again, his hands tightening against her.

The first touch of his blood on her tongue lit up her mind like fireworks.

The moment she swallowed, the whole world expanded, stretching into infinity and leaving her lost, a slave to the incredible feel of connecting with Antoine's mind through his blood. Strength flowed into her veins, carried by the heady and divine ambrosia she was greedily sucking down.

Heavens.

This man had the most powerful drug in the world flowing in his veins.

Her knees weakened.

She trembled but still kept drinking, needing a little more. She would stop before she went too far.

Sera worked her body against his, hungry for more than just blood. Antoine stiffened.

"Sera, stop," he said, voice deep and commanding, cutting through the haze in her mind. "Stop."

Why would she want to stop?

He tasted too damn good. She wanted to drink all of him. She wouldn't let him stop her. This was her blood. He would give it to her. She wouldn't let him refuse. If he did, she would show him what a foolish man he was to think he could deny her.

Good Christ.

Sera released his neck and recoiled, stumbling backwards and hitting the ebony corner post of the king-sized bed.

"Sera." Antoine rushed to her, his hands on her face and his voice soft and soothing. "Listen to me, Sera."

He stroked her cheeks, smoothing his palms over them. His hands were trembling and his neck was bloodied. Her stomach somersaulted and she swallowed.

How much had she taken? She had been drinking greedily, gulping down his blood.

"What?" she mumbled and tried to focus but her head spun violently, sending the room pitching and swaying. Her mind screamed for more blood. "The fuck?"

"Look at me, Sera," Antoine said and her eyes darted to his. They were blue again, beautiful and clear, and concerned. "It isn't your desire. Understand? Just ignore it and I will have it under control in a second."

He guided her to the bed before she could ask what he was talking about and forced her to sit on the edge.

Sera stared straight ahead. True to his word, the violent thoughts spinning through her mind began to disappear one by one, until her head was clear again and she no longer desired to tear Antoine's throat open as repayment for his audacity in thinking he could refuse her.

"Now you see the fire you play with?" Antoine's tone was dark.

He stood before her in only his black boxer shorts, as immense and powerful as Snow had looked earlier.

Dangerous.

"I tried to warn you." He turned away and Sera frowned at the wooden floorboards.

Bloodlust.

"It's contagious?" Her pulse spiked.

Had she just contracted bloodlust?

Antoine laughed, a bitter sound. "No. It wasn't your feelings. They were mine."

Her eyes widened. To think he endured that dark, deep mindless craving whenever he consumed blood.

"Not whenever," he said and she snapped her head around to look at him. He shrugged and gave her a forced smile. "I did not mean to pry. You consumed a large quantity of my blood. My family has always had the ability to read those weaker than us when they have enough of our blood in their body."

"I'm broadcasting my thoughts to you?"

He nodded. Well, that was certainly a new one on her.

Antoine sighed and sat beside her on the bed. "I do not intend to use it against you."

Something told her that he was talking about more than just reading her thoughts.

Could he control her too?

She had heard that some vampires, the older generation, possessed the ability to place vampires under their thrall, something which was normally reserved for humans only.

Was this how they did it, by having the vampire drink their blood?

"I feel dizzy." Sera flopped back onto the bed.

It was only when Antoine's gaze burned into her stomach and then her chest that she remembered she was naked. The cold chill in her blood burned away as she focused on Antoine, enjoying the feel of his eyes on her and the desire running rampant through her blood. He wanted her.

He lightly traced a line down her chest, between her breasts, and over her stomach to her navel. From there, he flattened his palm against her and continued downwards.

Sera rolled her eyes closed with the first brush of his fingers between her legs.

"Do you still wish to be tied up?" He sounded distinctly more interested in playing along with her now.

Not because he wanted to tie her up.

His blood in her body was broadcasting her thoughts and feelings to him. If she hadn't bitten him, he might have gone along with tying her up but he would have had to trust the feelings he was picking up in her and the things she said were the truth, not a cleverly constructed lie to make him believe that she trusted and didn't fear him.

Now, with his blood relaying everything to him and a connection between them that was wide open and showed no sign of closing any time soon, he would be able to feel the truth in her and she wouldn't be able to hide anything from him.

Sera nodded and raised her hands, placing her wrists together above her. She flicked her eyes opened and smiled into his, letting him feel everything that was flowing through her.

He really didn't scare her and she really did trust him, and this would prove it to him once and for all.

"Tie me up, Antoine."

CHAPTER 11

Antoine was one hundred and ten percent certain that this was a very bad idea.

Very, very bad.

Unfortunately, the raging hard-on in his boxers was telling him that he was in the mood for something very, very bad and what Sera proposed perfectly fit the bill. He couldn't think about her chained up and at his mercy without his cock twitching and aching.

The blood in her veins whispered that she wasn't lying about anything. She wanted this just as much as he did and she wasn't afraid, not even having experienced the rage of his bloodlust first hand. She was stronger than he had given her credit for and he was the first to admit that it pleased him.

Perhaps she could handle him and everything that entailed.

Still, he wasn't one to tempt fate so he rose from the bed, crossed the room to his chest of drawers and filled a glass with blood. He necked it and closed his eyes as it slid down his throat, replenishing some of what he had lost.

Just the memory of her mouth on his throat, his blood flowing into her, and the hungry sucking noises interspersed with muffled groans of pleasure had his erection straining against the black boxers. He wanted to sink his fangs into her as he drove his cock into her warmth, losing himself completely to his desire for this woman.

He had heard Javier and Callum as they passed his door this morning before he had fallen asleep. They had mentioned Sera and that he hadn't left his room since her arrival. The staff and performers would be talking about it too. He had missed a performance to be with her.

He had never missed a performance.

What was she doing to him?

There was a time when he would have killed anyone who tried to draw his blood, even those who had been close to him. He would have killed Anya. He had lived with her for a century and never once had he allowed her to taste him.

Sera had taken his blood twice now, once when healing him and just now when she had bitten him.

Bitten him.

Devil, he shouldn't want to risk awakening his bloodlust but he wanted to do it again.

The sharp sting of her fangs sinking into him and the rough pulls she had made on his blood had been ecstasy.

"Are you going to tie me up, Antoine?"

So husked his temptress. His wicked vixen.

She sat on the end of his bed, looking innocent even though she was nude, her blonde hair curling gracefully around her slender creamy shoulders and those mesmerising forest green eyes fixed on him in a challenge.

He never had been one to back down from a challenge.

Antoine smiled and crossed the room, holding her gaze all the while, letting her see that she was going to get her wish. He would do all in his power to control himself and not let his desire to bite her get the better of him. The blood he had just ingested would tide him over and keep the worst of his hunger at bay.

He picked up the discarded restraints and placed two next to her on the bed. The other two he held in one hand as he mounted the mattress.

Sera's gaze followed him.

He grabbed her wrist and effortlessly pulled her up the bed, so her head hit the crimson pillows, and then set about fastening the restraints around the bedposts.

He looped the chain around the carved black post, fastened the cuff at one end over it and snapped it shut.

The cuffs themselves weren't large enough to close around the post so it was the only way of securing them to his bed. It cut the chain short and he thanked fate for gifting him a small reprieve.

At least with her legs free, Sera could kick him if he took things too far and crossed a line.

He set the chain of the second restraint into the cuff of the one around the post and closed it, locking it tight. With the two sets joined, they reached where Sera lay and wouldn't pull too hard on her arms, giving her some room to move. He did the same with the remaining two cuffs, daisy-chaining them together.

"What about my feet?" Sera frowned at the restraints.

"It is probably best they are left free." Antoine could see she was going to protest and tell him to get another two sets off his brother so he killed it dead before it left her lips. "I might want to flip you on your front."

Her cheeks coloured deeply.

Beautiful.

He wanted to lick them and feel their heat whenever they did that. The sight of them made him want to say more wicked things so the blush spread and covered the whole of her body.

Sera stilled when he picked up the first cuff and placed it around her slender wrist.

They were designed to fit Snow's thicker wrists tightly so there was a gap around hers. If she tried hard enough, she would be able to slip her hand through the cuff and escape. That gave him peace of mind. He snapped the second one shut around her other wrist and then sat back.

Devil, she looked so good all chained to his bed and helpless.

Forget saying wicked things, he wanted to do bad things to her.

Very bad things.

His heart thumped against his breastbone, a heavy primal beat that had his blood pumping and carnal hunger creeping into his veins.

Sera wriggled on the bed and tugged at the restraints. Her little show almost did him in. He knew it was designed to reveal her vulnerability, to entice him, and by the Devil it worked.

He swooped on her mouth, covering her body with half of his, laying on her at an angle as he thrust his tongue past the barrier of her lips and claimed dominance over her.

She instantly arched into the kiss, body hot against his, her nipples hard points pressing into his chest. Her moan set him aflame, slicing away a fraction of his control, filling his head with thoughts of keeping her tied to his bed forever.

He didn't want to let her go.

This beautiful temptress, this wicked goddess, was his now and his alone. He wouldn't hurt her and he wouldn't allow her to hurt him.

His fingers tightened in her long blonde hair, dragging her head back and opening her mouth to him. She gasped and flinched but it didn't stop him. She was his. If she ever hurt him, he would...

Antoine pulled back and stared down at her. She lay beneath him, head held by his fierce grip on her hair, her deep green eyes wide.

Yet she felt no fear.

Only desire laced her blood.

He would never hurt her.

He loosened his grip, breathing hard and fighting for control. It didn't matter whether she hurt him. He would keep his promise. He would not force her to remain with him or seek vengeance.

"Antoine?" she whispered breathlessly. "Don't stop."

Antoine smoothed his hand over her cheek and stared into her eyes. He would never stop. If she let him, he would do this forever, even though part of him feared that forever would be taken from him once again. He didn't think he could survive if Sera did such a thing to him.

His brother had given him a reason to live last time, but if Sera left him, even Snow wouldn't be reason enough for him to remain.

"You look sad," she said.

He shook his head.

Grim, perhaps. Or afraid. But not sad. He could never be sad when he was looking at her. She had given him happiness the likes of which he had never experienced before.

These past few days with her had been Heaven.

"Kiss me, Antoine... make love to me."

That, he could most certainly do. He would never tire of pleasuring her because she gave him so much in return. Just seeing the pleasure painted across her beautiful face, the bliss he gave to her, was enough to satisfy him. When she touched him, placed her mouth on him or took him into her body and held onto him, it was nothing short of ecstasy.

He lowered his mouth and gently claimed her lips this time, a slow kiss intended to show her just how tender he could be with her. The bloodlust might lurk within him, commanding him to unleash his dark passions and take what he wanted from her, but he would never succumb to it. He would fight it for her.

Sera moaned and tangled her tongue with his, running the tip along the length and then curling it over the backs of his canines.

He growled and deepened the kiss, seeking more contact between them. His tongue swept over her teeth and his growl became a groan. Her fangs were out. His own canines lengthened in response and his eyes switched, his desire to taste her rearing up in his head again, driving him on.

Antoine broke away from her mouth and lowered his head to her breasts, sucking one nipple whilst he teased the other between his index finger and thumb, rolling the rosy bud with increasing hardness until Sera moaned. He pinched her nipple and she arched into him, her groan loud in the expansive room.

He didn't care if anyone heard them.

They were already talking about him and Sera.

They might as well hear the truth of it.

He sucked her nipple into his mouth and lightly bit. The taste of blood spread through his mouth and saliva pooled, his hunger for her rising. He sucked on the small scratch where his fangs had caught her, his body tightening with each breathy moan she loosed and each tiny molecule of blood he took.

She trusted him.

He had never doubted that.

But he didn't trust himself.

He kissed down from her breasts, running his hands over her soft supple flesh, devouring her stomach with wet open-mouthed kisses that had her moaning and writhing. Antoine looked up at her as he kissed and licked her, needing to see her restrained and using the sight of her bound and at his mercy to heighten everything he was feeling.

Sera tipped her head back and groaned.

His eyes fixed on the tight cords of her neck. He stared at them and licked her stomach, sucked it until she gasped and he smelt the blood breaking beneath the surface of her skin.

"Antoine," she moaned and raised her hips, forcing her stomach up to his mouth.

He dragged his lips away from her and gently kissed the black welt just a few inches above her hip.

A love bite.

How very human of him.

He could give her a better love bite than that.

Everything burned red and he struck without thinking, slamming his fangs hard into her hip.

Sera bucked and shrieked, her body trembling beneath him. The scent of her desire flooded the room, mixing with the taste of her blood as he swallowed little more than a single mouthful before pulling away from her.

He licked the bite mark, damning himself for biting her but congratulating himself for remaining conscious enough that he had been able to stop at just one small taste.

Devil, Sera did taste good though and he wanted another bite.

Sera moaned as he licked the bite mark and he felt her eyes on him.

His gaze slid to hers but he didn't stop licking, taking every drop that seeped from the cuts as they began to heal. She still wasn't afraid. The acceptance in her soft look, mixed with a heavy dose of desire, told him that she would allow him to bite her again if he wanted to, regardless of the danger to herself.

He wanted to kiss her for that.

He settled for kissing the bite mark on her hip. His mark. He had never bitten someone before.

Was she his now?

In the old days, a mark like this had been considered a claim. That tradition had long died out but he was ancient enough to remember it and part of him still clung to the old ways. He pressed his lips to the mark and then kissed downwards, following the line of her hip to the neat pale curls that covered her groin.

She moaned and struggled against the restraints as he parted her thighs and settled himself between them. The thought of sinking his cock into her welcoming heat had him close to surrendering to that desire but he held himself back, intent on pleasuring her first and satisfying his own need second.

He lowered himself and spread her soft plush petals, opening her to his gaze. She glistened with moisture, the sight of her so ready for him and the scent of her desire stirring his own.

He closed his eyes, reached his tongue out, and quickly stroked it over her clitoris.

She moaned and arched into the touch, and he had to see her. He opened his eyes again and watched her as he licked her, teasing her with his tongue, drinking the sweet honey of her arousal as he drank in the sight of her pleasure. It flickered across her face and in his blood, pure and honest, deep and fathomless.

Pleasure he had stirred in her.

An arrow of pride shot through him and he licked her harder, settled his mouth over the aroused nub and suckled it.

Sera groaned again, tipping her head back and clamping her thighs down on him, squeezing his head between them. He eased her legs apart and continued, studying her reactions, searching for the movements that had her panting the hardest and had desire burning up her blood.

She tensed and gasped when he eased two fingers into her core, settling them there. His cock throbbed with the memory of how she felt wrapped around it, so wet and inviting, gloving him perfectly.

He wanted to be inside her again, possessing her and showing her that she belonged to him now and he intended to fill the rest of their years with bliss.

Sera writhed on his fingers, riding them in a way that sent his hunger and arousal soaring.

So wanton and wicked.

She was beautiful as she sought her pleasure, her face alternating between a hard frown and a soft sigh, her hands tightly closed around the chains of her restraints. His cock pulsed against the mattress and his stomach, balls tightening as he absorbed the vision of her chained and giving herself over to passion.

"More," she whispered and he resisted the temptation to point out that she was the one riding his fingers.

He wasn't moving at all, was simply holding them fast within her while he lavished her clitoris with his attentive tongue. She groaned and twisted, wrists tugging at the restraints, and her movements roughened, hips shifting harder and faster.

Antoine suckled her and gave her one single thrust of his fingers.

She screamed out her climax, hips jerking off the mattress, and he didn't release her. He kept pumping and licking her, teasing her until she begged him to stop, whispering that she couldn't take any more.

Antoine withdrew his fingers and licked them, savouring the taste of her desire.

Sera's green eyes slowly opened and she frowned and licked her lips.

His cock jumped.

She smiled wickedly, an inviting one that said she didn't need a connection between their blood for her to know what he wanted to do.

Antoine moved up the length of her, kissing and licking, body tightening with each inch closer he moved to her mouth. He covered it with his when he reached it, plunging his tongue in deep and unleashing his passion. It was rough but she matched him strength for strength, her tongue battling his and her breathy moans driving him on.

She nipped at his lower lip, sucked it into her mouth, and swept her tongue over it in a way that sent sparks of pleasure rippling through him. He wanted to bite her when she did that, wanted her to bite him, craved the feel of her teeth sinking into his lip and giving him the ultimate bliss.

He broke away from her mouth and kissed along her jaw.

When she had caught her breath, he knelt astride her chest.

Her green eyes dropped to his cock and he looked down at her wrists, the sight of them bound heating his blood and pushing him to go through with it. She wanted it too, knew what was coming and hadn't refused him.

Antoine moved up her and gripped the top of the headboard with one hand.

He ran his other hand down his cock, revealing the crown, and then poised himself above her mouth.

Her lips parted, her gaze locked on his, pupils blown and eyes rich with desire and need.

Antoine groaned and tightly grasped his cock, the hint of pain only adding to his pleasure along with the intoxicating thought of what was to come.

He lowered his erection, slowly sliding it into her hot mouth, and groaned as she wrapped her lips around him. His hand left his rigid length and joined the one that had a death-grip on the headboard. He closed his eyes and then opened them again, forcing himself to watch Sera beneath him, her mouth around his length.

Trusting him.

Antoine slowly raised his hips and then eased back into her mouth, setting a pace that wouldn't hurt her but would have him coming undone before long. She moaned with each deep thrust of his cock, throat vibrating against the sensitive head, and he groaned with her, breathless and lost to the sensations.

He tried to keep his movements steady and gentle, but faltered at times. She groaned whenever he thrust deeper and it was hard to resist the urge to keep that rougher pace rather than return to a softer one.

He stared down at her. The sight of her beneath him, eyes closed as she sucked his cock and grasped the chains of her restraints, added to the potent pleasure flowing in his blood. The occasional scrape of her teeth over his length tore deep rumbling groans from him and had him closing his eyes and hanging his head, shaking all over and his breath trembling as he fucked her pretty mouth.

His hands shook against the headboard, claws puncturing the black wood, and he pumped into her, backside tensing with each slow careful thrust.

He couldn't take any more.

His balls tightened, drawing up, and he groaned. "Sera."

He jerked to a halt and the heat in his blood burst into flames that engulfed him, sending hot sparks skittering over his skin. The rush of his seed leaving him, the thought of it filling Sera's mouth as she swallowed around him, had him crying out her name and collapsing into the headboard. He struggled to hold himself above her, weak from his climax, hazy with it and the gentle way that Sera lapped at him.

Antoine rolled to one side, landing on the mattress with his back against her arm and breathed hard to gather himself. His cock twitched, still hard and aching for more. Aching for Sera. He wouldn't be satisfied until he had pumped his seed into her, claiming her in the most primal of ways.

She gasped when he shifted between her legs, nothing more than a flash of cold air, hooked her knees over his shoulders and plunged his cock into her slick core.

"Antoine," she moaned as he slowly withdrew, letting her feel the full length of him and what she did to him.

He wanted to be gentle with her but he couldn't. The need to claim her was too fierce. He grasped her hips, buried his face against her knee and thrust into her, long and deep, rough and fast. She curled her pelvis and hooked her feet around his neck.

Antoine growled.

His beautifully wicked girl.

She moaned with each hard plunge of his body into hers, quivering beneath him, tempting him to surrender completely to his true nature. He could claim more than her body.

He could claim all of her.

His eyes flicked open.

Her pale slender neck was within easy reach if he thrust a little deeper.

She cried out when he did, burying himself to the hilt with each stroke, and her legs fell down his arms again, freeing him and allowing him to reach her throat.

He leaned over her, hands planted either side of her breasts, gaze locked on the pulse flickering just above her left collarbone. He drove into her, grunting with each meeting of their hips, possessing her just as he had wanted.

"Please, Antoine," she whispered and he was lost in her, in the feel of her body straining against his, their sweat sticking their skin together as he pumped her, pushing her towards another climax.

He would make this one the best she had ever had.

He would ruin her to all others.

Antoine's lips peeled back off his fangs and he stared at her throat, thrust harder and faster into her, savouring her moans and breathy sighs, waiting for the right moment.

She clenched him, her body squeezing and releasing, driving him on. She was made for him. Whether it would be as his downfall or as his saviour was yet to be seen, but she was made for him.

He growled and pumped her deeper, hips pistoning, his grunts a dark sound compared with her softer moans.

"Antoine," she murmured and thrashed her head away from him, the muscles in her arms straining as she pulled on her restraints. "Yes... oh, yes."

Antoine sucked in a deep breath and sank his fangs hard into her throat at the same moment as his cock thrust to the hilt inside her.

Sera screamed his name at the top of her lungs, the sound like Heaven to his ears, and her body tensed and then exploded into a wild throbbing around him, discordant to the pulses and tremors of his own orgasm.

He drank deeply as he spilled himself inside her, claiming all of her.

She belonged to him now.

Her bliss ran through the connection between them and he knew she would feel his own as their minds joined. Tiny pinpricks of glowing light, a dazzling array of colours, punctured the usual darkness of his mind and grew to illuminate the endless gloom.

Antoine slowed his drinking and frowned.

He hadn't lost control.

He sealed the cuts with a sweep of his tongue and then drew back and looked down at Sera.

She opened her beautiful green eyes, her breathing rough and fast. He stroked her cheek and she met his gaze, hers full of so much affection and warmth. He knew the depth of her feelings. He could see them in her eyes, her heart on display, and feel them in her blood and they didn't frighten him.

They flattered him, humbled him.

He had promised that he would never hurt her and she had trusted him even when he had feared that he wouldn't be able to keep that promise.

He had though.

Her deep growing affection for him, the warmth she showed to him in every action, every kiss and smile she gave to him, had given him the strength he needed.

He had subdued his darker side and kept it at bay without even trying.

Antoine lowered his mouth to kiss her.

"Can you take these off now?" Sera rattled the chains.

He had forgotten about them.

"Are they hurting you?" He inspected one of her wrists, running his thumb over the smooth unmarked skin.

"No."

Antoine looked back at her and she smiled wickedly.

"I just want to use them on you now."

Antoine grinned and undid her wrist.

Devil, he could go along with that.

CHAPTER 12

Sera was gentle as she settled her palm against his bare chest. Antoine followed her silent instruction, kneeling back on the bed as she rose towards him. She curled her legs around beside her, tucking her feet beneath her bottom, and stroked a line down his chest. He closed his eyes and inhaled slowly, heart pounding against her palm, nerves rising.

Snow reacted violently whenever Antoine set restraints on him. Antoine wasn't sure how he would react when Sera closed the heavy steel and leather cuffs around his wrists and secured him to the bed. He refused to listen to the fear at the back of his mind, the whispered poisonous words that said he would react as violently as Snow did and would hurt her.

He wouldn't.

She had made herself vulnerable in order to show him the depth of her trust and her belief in him, and he wanted to do the same for her.

What if he did have an adverse reaction though? The black carved wooden pillars of his four-poster bed would snap like tinder if he used all of his strength on them. He would easily escape.

"You don't have to do this," Sera whispered and ran her fingers over his chest, her eyes soft with understanding and concern.

A hint of desire remained in them though.

She liked the thought of tying him up, and Devil he liked it too.

For the first time in his life, he wanted to be chained and restrained. He wanted to give over control to someone else.

"I do." Antoine leaned in, snaked his right hand around the back of Sera's head, tunnelling his fingers into her hair, and drew her to him. His gaze dropped to her mouth and his heart thudded, a heavy beat that rocked him and made his breath shudder. He closed his eyes, claimed her sweet lips and kissed her as softly as he could manage. When she leaned into the kiss, he pulled away and stared down at her. Her eyelids lifted, revealing deep green irises and wide aroused pupils. "I want to do this."

She nodded, shifted her hand to his cheek and stroked it, her touch as soft as feathers and teasing his senses.

Would she be that gentle with him when she had him chained and at her mercy?

Sweet Hell, he hoped that she was.

He enjoyed the times when they were rough and wicked with each other, but it was the times when they were gentle and tender that reached right down to his soul and deeply affected him.

"Lie down," Sera husked, the vixen in her surfacing.

Her smile was wicked as he obeyed and sprawled out on his back on the red covers, his head on the pillows.

Antoine drew in a deep steadying breath and stretched his arms across the pillows. His heart continued to pound, blood rushing as his gaze followed Sera's every move.

She knelt next to his right arm, carefully lifted his wrist and placed it in the cradle of the cuff. He inhaled another deep breath as she closed the cuff around his wrist. It fit snugly, no room around his wrist for him to wriggle and get his hand through should he want to escape.

His only option would be to smash the bedposts.

Easy enough to do. He just hoped it didn't come to that. He liked his bed.

Panic closed his throat and Sera paused, as though she had sensed the spike in his emotions. She probably had. His blood still flowed in her veins, enough of it that he could feel her emotions clearly but could no longer hear her thoughts. She would be able to feel him through that connection too. She stroked his arm, soft and tender, soothing his panic until he felt he could breathe again.

"We really don't have—"

"I want to," Antoine interjected and she nodded but didn't look sure. He sighed. "I am just concerned that I might not react well. I do not want to hurt you."

"I know." She leaned over and pressed a kiss to the inside of his elbow, and then worked her way up his arm, paying close attention to any scar she came across.

He loved when she kissed them because he felt the compassion in her with each press of her lips, the deep affection that she hid in her heart, affection that matched the feelings that lurked in his, held beyond the reach of her sight.

She drew back and frowned down at him, and he had a hard time not staring at her bare breasts. The dark plum buds of her nipples called to him and he wanted to grab her and drag her down to him so he could suckle them.

"If you panic... Snow will feel you, won't he?" There was worry in her eyes now.

Antoine smiled. "Most likely, although he does know we have the restraints and your intentions when asking him for them was very clear. There is a chance he would not come bursting through the door and catch us in the act."

A beautiful deep crimson coloured her cheeks and she cast her gaze downwards, settling it on his chest.

Antoine's smile widened.

"I will do my best to relax. I am sure it is just fear of the unknown and once I am bound, I will be more comfortable."

Sera nodded again and went to crawl over the top of him. Antoine grabbed her around the back of her neck with his free hand, dragged her down to him and kissed her.

She moaned into his mouth, her whole body tense, and then relaxed into him. The feel of her soft warm skin on his tore a groan from his throat and he deepened the kiss, claiming her lips and bruising them with his force. He needed to kiss her like this, to taste her and devour her, to dominate her before she dominated him.

Everything male in him said to make it clear right now who was in charge and that she was his.

Antoine growled when he tried to wrap his other arm around her and felt the tug of the restraint.

Sera bit his lower lip and then sat back, a smile on her face. "Sucks, doesn't it? I wanted to touch you so badly when you had me tied up. I ached to place my hands on you."

He growled again, low and feral, aroused by the thought of desiring something he couldn't do.

She wasn't exactly encouraging him to go along with letting her tie his other wrist up.

The thought of not being able to touch her was torture to him.

He wanted to ghost his hands over every inch of her flawless pale skin and kiss her from head to toe, something he couldn't do with his hands bound.

He went to grab her again but she evaded his hand, caught his wrist, and had it pinned to the pillows next to the cuff before he could blink.

Antoine relaxed into the bed and let her have her way. He could easily escape her grasp but part of him didn't want to—the part that wanted to experience what Sera had said and was aroused by the thought of being bound and helpless.

She took his hand, settled his wrist in the cuff and closed it.

Antoine felt her tense.

He tensed too, waiting to feel something crash over him. Panic. Fear. Rage.

Nothing came.

He looked at his bound left hand and then at his right. The sight of them sent a hot rush of arousal through his veins. His arms were longer than Sera's so there was some slack in the chains but he could only raise them a few inches off the pillows. He tugged at them, curled his arms as much as he could, testing their strength.

"None of that." Sera mounted his chest. She knelt astride him, took hold of his forearms and pressed them down into the crimson pillows, forcing him to relax. "You'll break them and I'm not asking Snow for another set."

Antoine raised an eyebrow at her. He wouldn't break the restraints. He'd had them built to withstand Snow's strength. It was more likely that the bed would snap rather than the chains, and restraints would be useless then.

Unless she locked his hands together behind his back.

Antoine shouldn't have liked the image that popped into his mind with that thought, but the idea of lying with his hands chained behind his back and Sera on top of him had his desire soaring. His cock twitched and began to harden again. He tugged at his restraints, gentler this time so Sera didn't reprimand him, and groaned at the feel of them.

Sera giggled.

"I think you're enjoying this more than I thought you would." She reached over behind her and ran her hand down his hard length, tearing another moan from him.

The feel of her sitting astride his chest, her heat seeping into him, and her hand on his cock was exquisite. He rolled his eyes closed with the next stroke of her hand down his length and then opened them again, staring deep into hers. She held his gaze, hers soft and full of desire, passionate and intense.

She ran her hands along his arms and shifted backwards. He groaned and swallowed, tried to keep his eyes locked with hers as she moved down his body, trailing her fingers over his chest and then his stomach. He pulled at the restraints, moaning as they bit into his wrists, the spark of pain intensifying his pleasure.

"Antoine," Sera whispered and his attention snapped back to her.

She ran her fingertips in circles around his nipples and then down over the ridges of his stomach. He tensed it for her, eliciting a sweet moan. She traced each muscle, fingers following the dips between them, her tongue sweeping over her lower lip.

He stared at her mouth, wanting to kiss her when she did that.

She leaned over and replaced her fingers with her lips, kissing him instead, sweeping her mouth over his stomach. She shuffled backwards, knees astride his thighs, and licked the hollow of his navel.

He laughed.

Her answering giggle was light and soft, and she swirled her tongue around his navel again.

Antoine bucked up, the cuffs tight against his wrists, and laughed harder. His stomach tensed and flipped, fluttering. He never should have revealed his weakness. She was merciless as she teased it, her giggling and his laughter mingling and lightening the mood for a brief few seconds.

When she sat back, her eyes met his and the mood changed again, deepening once more.

With his blood in her body, it was impossible for her to hide her feelings from him, but the fact that she wasn't even trying touched him and drew him into responding in kind.

He stared into her eyes and let his feelings bubble to the surface so she would see them in his eyes and feel them in his blood.

Her cheeks flushed again and he smiled at her, soft and warm, content beneath her even though he was bound and powerless.

He had been bound and powerless from the moment he had met her.

Sera moved up him, grasped his cock and positioned it beneath her. She held his gaze as she slowly sank down on it, drawing him into her heat and stealing his breath away.

He struggled to focus, switching between wanting to close his eyes and revel in the feel of her body encasing his, and staring into her eyes and drowning in their combined feelings.

Sera settled her hands against his stomach and rose off him, as slowly as she had sunk onto him. He groaned and she joined him, her moan so low that he barely heard her.

His arms tensed, body going rigid as she began to ride him, setting a pace that threatened to overwhelm him. His emotions slipped beyond his control, rising to the surface, all of them there in his eyes and his heart for her to see. He had expected the cuffs to make him vulnerable but not like this.

It felt as though she was drawing his feelings out of him through his eyes as she stared into them, deep and intense, her own full of emotions that echoed the ones beating in his heart.

He groaned and sighed, frowned.

Her slow tempo drove him crazy, deepening the connection between them until he lost awareness of their surroundings and could only focus on Sera as she pressed her hands into his stomach, tipped her head back, and rode his cock.

Her breathy moans were music to his ears, adding to his ecstasy and pushing him towards the edge.

Antoine couldn't stop himself from groaning each time she slid down his cock and took him back into her body, tightly gloving him, heating him to his core. He kept still beneath her, letting her be the one in control, knowing that if he did she would give him the ultimate pleasure.

Her gaze held his, warm with affection but edged with fear. He felt that same fear in his heart, a whisper at the back of his mind that warned this was dangerous. He was falling for her and no good would come of it.

Antoine didn't care.

Fear meant nothing in this moment. The future meant nothing. All he could focus on was the present, the intense connection blossoming between them as their bodies joined in a mutual search for pleasure.

Antoine had never felt anything like it.

It was mind-blowing, incredible, and shook him to his soul. He had never experienced such a connection with anyone, not in all the years he had been alive and all the relationships he'd had.

He needed more.

"Sera," he husked and she bit her lip, her pupils widening, as though the sound of him saying her name aroused her and heightened her pleasure.

He tipped his head back, silently trying to tell her where he wanted her. He craved the feel of her mouth on his, her taste flooding him. He needed to complete the connection between them through a kiss.

She moaned and ran her hands up his chest, her strokes faltering, quickening. Antoine pumped his hips, meeting her on each down stroke, tearing another throaty blissful moan from her. She leaned over him and he craned his neck, caught her lips and kissed her.

Ecstasy.

Did she feel it too?

He tugged at his restraints, mentally cursing them. He wanted to clutch her to him and hold her, keep her moving on him while he kissed her.

She took control of the kiss, using his distraction against him, and he melted into the pillow. Her tongue swept past his lips to tangle with his, her sweet taste flooding his mouth. Her slow thrusts drove him out of his mind, the pleasure too intense, and he felt as though he was going to scream or explode.

He wanted release, needed to feel her quiver with her climax, desperately desired to thrust his cock hard into her and spill himself.

"Sera," he whispered, one half pleading her to give him release and the other half begging her to continue and draw it out for as long as possible.

He didn't want to lose this incredible connection to her, this soul-deep joining of their bodies and their emotions. Whatever they had, it was a rare thing, one he wouldn't give up, not for anything or anyone.

"Antoine," she moaned into his mouth and her fingers tightened against his shoulders, nails pressing in and adding a spark of pain to the bliss burning through him.

She groaned and moved faster, harder, driving down onto his cock and choking him in her depths. Still not enough.

He dug his heels into the mattress and pumped her, rocking his cock into her hot sheath. Her moans were exquisite, so full of pleasure and need. Two feelings he awoke in her and was more than happy to fulfil.

She tangled her hands in his hair, kissing him deeper, and it felt as though she was taking all of him into her, and giving all of herself to him.

He pulled at his restraints again, frustrated, desperate to touch her and hold her to him, to roll her over onto her back and drive into her.

She tightened around him, trembled and then bit down hard on his lip as her body jerked forwards. Her body clenched him and throbbed, milking his cock, and his orgasm crashed over him. He lifted his hips off the bed, pushing himself deep into her core as he climaxed, flooding her with his seed.

Sera was still a moment, teeth clamped down on his lower lip, body shaking around his, and then relaxed. He closed his eyes and exhaled on a heavy sigh, heat running through his limbs and carrying his strength away.

She kissed along his jaw and down his neck, and Antoine didn't have the strength to deny her. He tipped his head to one side and groaned her name as she sank her fangs deep into his throat.

Bliss.

Fiery, consuming, and so intense that he trembled.

He moaned with each soft pull she made, drawing his blood to her, sending his head spinning. Her hands clutched his shoulders, squeezed, held him in a way that said she wouldn't let him go either.

Her soft suckling filled his ears as her feelings flooded his mind. The connection that had opened between them when they had been making love was nothing compared to the one that sprang into life now, filling his mind with bright colours and endless warmth.

"Sera," he whispered, a plea this time.

He didn't want her to stop.

He could hold the darkness at bay for her, would never let it touch her mind again.

He wanted every time they made love to end like this, with sharing blood.

He craved the connection to her.

She sucked harder and he couldn't take it. The feel of her hands on him, her lips on his throat and her fangs in his body, his blood flowing into her, and their bodies intimately entwined was so profound and erotic that it overwhelmed him.

His cock stiffened, balls ached, and a second orgasm rocked him, far stronger than the first and so unexpected that it sent his head spinning towards fathomless darkness. Towards unconsciousness.

Sera moaned as he pumped his seed into her again and her body shuddered. Her fangs left his throat and she breathed hard against his neck, her sheath milking him once more. The feel of her climaxing with him because of their connection and sharing blood had him reaching for her but the cuffs bit into his wrists, reminding him that he wasn't able to do what he wanted.

Sera relaxed against him, hands shaking on his shoulders, breath trembling across his chest.

When her bite had sent him careening towards passing out, he had feared that she had awakened his bloodlust, but he felt none of the effects. He felt hazy and warm, at peace and one with her. Sera. His seducer. His vixen. His goddess.

Her thoughts swam in his mind and he tried not to listen to them, but their subject and her emotions tugged at his heart.

She feared.

She was afraid that he would leave her someday, that she would lose the incredible man beneath her. He would have smiled at being called incredible had it not been for the fact that her fear was genuine, and ran deep in her heart. She feared he would be taken from her and that she wouldn't be able to stop it from happening.

It wasn't the bloodlust that she feared, but him leaving her for another woman—the woman he had almost forgotten.

Sera had chased Anya from his mind and his heart, but now she had brought her back again, a ghost that haunted him and one he had thought he had freed himself from.

He wanted to tell Sera that she had no reason to fear because he would never leave her but he had promised not to use the blood connection between them to pry. She would never forgive him if he revealed that he had listened in on her private thoughts.

Antoine needed to do something to reassure her though. The need was primal, controlling, a male desire to protect his female and ensure her happiness and comfort.

He growled and pulled at the cuffs that bound him, muscles rippling and body going rigid.

Sera lifted her head, her green eyes wide, shock echoing in them.

Not fear. She didn't think he had lost his mind to bloodlust then.

He silently thanked her for her faith in him and pulled his wrists towards him. The cuffs at the other end of the ones that held him began to bend. He tugged harder, straining and growling, and they crumpled under the pressure and slipped through the cuffs of the restraints attached to the bedposts.

The sudden release of pressure against his wrists was something he probably should have anticipated. His left fist smashed into the side of his face and the mangled cuff still attached to it flipped over his face and smacked him in the ear. His other fist cracked against it, driving the metal against his head.

Pain buzzed across his skull.

Antoine didn't care.

He grabbed a startled Sera, wrapped his arms around her and dragged her down against him. He kissed her with every ounce of feeling that beat for her in his dark heart, hoping to show her without words that she had nothing to fear.

She melted into him, her palms against his chest, her kisses soft and light, full of need and affection.

Antoine held her closer, drawing her deeper into his embrace.

He would never leave her.

No one on this Earth could take him from her.

No one.

CHAPTER 13

Antoine was on edge. Sera was back in his room, showering and dressing for the evening.

Dressing.

He couldn't remember the last time he had worn clothes. It felt like weeks ago rather than the days it must have been.

Javier had slipped a note under his door this morning, reminding him that he had an appointment before tonight's party. The two male elite vampires he was meeting were the reason for the party, and one of them was the reason Javier was so insistent that he show his face.

Javier's younger brother, Andreu, would be covering for him while he was on extended leave for six months to train Lilah in being a vampire and honeymooning with her after their impending nuptials.

The other newcomer to the theatre was from a family that were a close acquaintance of Callum's. Callum had assured him that Payne would be a suitable substitute while he was on paternity leave.

Antoine raked his fingers through his dark hair. Devil. If someone had told him one hundred years ago that the dedicated bachelors who had approached him about opening an erotic theatre would end up besotted and married off, he would have laughed and told them to pull the one with bells on.

He hadn't seen this one coming.

He hadn't seen Sera coming either.

"And this is the main stage," Javier said, Spanish accent thick now that he had been in the company of his brother for a day solid.

His voice echoed around the empty theatre.

Andreu cast his deep blue gaze over the black stage and the red velvet couches that made up the set. If it hadn't been for those eyes, so different to Javier's rich brown ones, and the darker shade of his brown hair, the two of them might have been twins. Javier was barely half an inch taller than his brother was, and both had wide shoulders that filled the breadth of their black designer suits.

Payne was a contrast to both of them. He wore his dirty blond hair cropped close to the sides of his head and spiked on top, and wore black jeans with his pinstriped black shirt. The rolled-up sleeves hugged his toned forearms close to his elbows and revealed an elaborate array of tattoos on their undersides, intricate symbols that had caught Antoine's attention the moment he had met the young vampire.

And he had eyes that Antoine had discovered were unpleasant to look into for any lengthy period of time.

They looked dull slate grey in the low light coming from the stage but back in Antoine's office, they had shone with the eeriest flecks of amber and blue.

The background checks Antoine had run on their two newest employees hadn't revealed anything unusual, especially where Payne was concerned.

In fact, his file was so clean that Antoine suspected the man made a serious amount of effort to stay off the radar.

Even Andreu's had revealed a few fights and some dark business dealings. Javier had vouched for his brother though and Antoine believed him when he said that Andreu was completely devoted to this position and the work it entailed and wouldn't be a problem.

Andreu was completely devoted to business full stop.

Antoine could see it in the way he assessed everything, from the furnishings to the staff.

Here was a man dedicated to making money, and lots of it, and God forbid anything tried to get in his way. He reminded Antoine of himself as a youth.

Andreu was probably the same age as he had been back when his mind had been more on fast money and pleasure than anything of real worth.

Payne looked across his broad muscled shoulders as the double doors behind Antoine opened.

Callum.

Antoine didn't need to look to know the young elite vampire had just walked in with a few performers tailing him.

He kept his gaze on Payne, intrigued by the way the coloured flecks in his eyes pierced the darkness in the moment before he turned his head away and fixed his gaze back on Javier.

Interesting.

Coupled with the tattoos and his all-too-clean background, it was enough to stir Antoine's curiosity.

But not enough to keep his mind off his apartment and Sera.

Javier continued his tour and Antoine didn't bother to follow them. He had met the males and had spent enough time with them. His concern shifted to Callum now. The black-haired elite male slouched into one of the front row seats and waved a hand at the performers on the stage. The trio immediately set into action, the two men stripping the woman, slowly peeling her clothes off and kissing each inch of skin they exposed.

"Are we hiring her?" Callum said and Antoine frowned, lost for a moment. "Elizabeth's youngling."

"Devil, no," Antoine muttered and sat next to him in one of the red velvet seats. "If she even tries to get on that stage you are to come and tell me, understand?"

"Javier said you would respond with something like that." Callum's green eyes stayed fixed on the performers as they began to go through the more erotic side of their routine.

He couldn't fool Antoine.

The elite vampire radiated tension, from his aura to the way he kept picking at the arm of the seat, intent on fraying the fabric.

"How did the scan go?" Antoine spoke low enough that the three performers wouldn't hear.

Callum swallowed.

"Um, well... she is definitely pregnant." He tapped his fingers on the seat arm now, his tension mounting.

Any moment now, he was going to explode. Why?

Callum shot around to face him, his eyes bright and wide. "Apparently we're expecting twins."

Ah. Antoine could see why that might be a problem. Two mixed breeds were more difficult to hide and protect from the uglier side of their world than one.

"I am sure that nothing bad will befall them, Callum. I would be more than happy to have them at the theatre. Kristina is welcome here any time she wishes to come. She would be safer here." There was a time, probably little more than a few days ago, when he would have been surprised to hear himself saying such a thing to an elite, or any vampire.

He smiled to himself.

Not anymore.

Sera had shown him that allowing others into his life wasn't a bad thing and that company was good for his soul, and for his bloodlust. It was better to let his emotions out than struggle to keep them contained.

Callum was family, and so was Javier, and that bond extended to those the two elite males loved.

"I know she would," Callum said on a sigh. "I am trying to convince her to come and stay in my apartment here, but she's still not sure. She feels The Langham hotel is safer with all the humans around her. No vampire or werewolf would dare cause a ruckus in such a public place."

"When the twins are born though—"

"I will have her move here. I will not let my children come to harm, and I know you will protect them."

"Will they be hybrids?" Antoine had never heard of hybrids being born of a union between a vampire and a werewolf. He had heard tales of mixed couples producing offspring but normally those couples went into hiding and were never seen again.

Callum hesitated but then relief blossomed in his eyes. "No. Apparently not. The doctor has said that one will be born vampire and one born werewolf. One hundred percent. No crossover at all."

Relief washed through Antoine too. "I am glad. It will be far easier to protect them, especially if their parentage remains anonymous. No one need know they were born of a vampire and a werewolf unless they wished to reveal it."

"Javier was right."

Antoine frowned. "About what?"

"She is good for you." Callum grinned.

Antoine huffed. "That is yet to be seen."

"I'm seeing it right now. The Antoine I left to audition Sera wouldn't have sat here with me discussing babies." Callum's grin cracked even wider. "I presume you've been taking precautions in this love affair of yours?"

"Precautions?" Antoine blinked when it hit him. "Sera is not in heat. I would know if she was receptive."

Callum laughed. "You would if she were an aristocrat."

Antoine's blood drained downwards and froze.

Callum laughed louder, drawing the attention of the three vampires on the stage, and clapped a hand down hard on his shoulder.

"I'm just kidding. Elite still have mating cycles, just like the aristocrats."

Antoine rose from his seat and scowled at him. "I find your jokes quite distasteful. It is no wonder I have never taken the time to share a glass of blood with you."

"Come on, Antoine," Callum said but he cut him off with a glare. A reminder. Callum held his hands up and sighed in resignation. "Fine, I get it. You're still the boss... no bad jokes."

Antoine huffed again and stormed towards the double doors that led backstage, intent on heading to his office there and finding some peace so he could get his head straight at last.

Sera was under his skin, intoxicated him whenever he was near her, but he still had his doubts about her and what he was doing.

It would be too easy to go along with whatever was happening between them, blindly sinking deeper into something that could end up destroying him.

Anya stood at the back of his mind and in his heart, a shadowy reminder that things he thought were going well could so easily go wrong.

"Antoine," Callum called out and he stopped and looked back over his shoulder. "Thank you for everything though. I really do appreciate it."

Antoine nodded and pushed the doors open. They swung shut behind him, closing with enough force that the sound echoed around the black-walled double-height room.

What if Callum was wrong about mating cycles?

He frowned.

A thousand years old was too young for starting a family, especially with one who was probably not a day over thirty.

It wasn't just the nine hundred odd years' age gap that kept his blood cold in his veins though.

Bloodlust was genetic.

He would pass it on to any children he might produce.

The desire to be alone intensified but he ignored it, knowing what he really needed to soothe the tempest in his mind, and climbed the stairs to the second floor where his apartment and those of his three friends were.

He paused outside his mahogany panelled door and then continued along the black and gold hallway to Snow's.

"Enter," Snow said before he even had time to knock. He twisted the brass knob and pushed the door open, revealing Snow reclining on the black covers of his bed in only his boxer shorts and an open black robe. "I wondered how long it would be before you came to check on me. You spiked a few minutes ago. Did Callum say something upsetting?"

Antoine would never get used to the incredible strength of his brother's senses. It always astounded him when his brother told him everywhere he had been and who he had been speaking with while there.

He closed the door and crossed the wooden floor to Snow's bed. Snow settled his open book on his stomach, pages face down.

Antoine's gaze flicked to it. War and Peace. A little light reading.

The spine was cracked and worn.

He would need to buy Snow a new copy soon.

He wasn't sure how many times Snow had read it now, or how he could stand to read the same novels over and over again when there were so many new ones out there.

Snow liked the classics though.

Antoine could remember his brother reading to him when he was a toddler, telling him Nordic stories of incredible gods and worlds beyond the imagination, and tales of things he had seen during his travels.

Snow was more than just a brother to him.

He had been like a father too, the age gap between them meaning that Snow had been fully grown long before Antoine had been born. Snow had raised him with his mother, leaving their father free to focus on his business and on protecting their entire family.

"How is your female?" Snow gave him an expectant look.

Antoine hadn't come here to talk about her but he couldn't help himself now that his brother had mentioned her.

He sat on the edge of the bed, side on to Snow, and rubbed his hand over his face and then his dark hair, trying to think about where to start.

"She is well... excited about the party tonight."

"Something is troubling you, Brother." Snow sat up and placed his book on the ebony bedside table. Antoine noticed the chafing on his wrist as the sleeve of his silk robe rode up his arm. Snow smiled. "Do not worry about me too. You have enough worries. You fear she will hurt you."

Antoine had never been able to hide anything from his brother. Not his monumental joy at having found a woman he had thought would become his eternal mate, and not his crushing agony on discovering that she had disappeared without a trace.

"You feel everything so keenly." Snow propped himself up on his right elbow. "Sometimes your feelings cannot be trusted though, Antoine."

"What do you mean?" He frowned and looked across his shoulder at his brother.

Snow sighed and combed his fingers through his white hair, preening it back from his face. His pale eyes were like clear winter skies, no spot of cloud marring them.

Antoine's own eyes held pale flakes like snow and he had always thought his brother deserved them more than he did. They would have suited him.

A vampire liked mystery and it was something Snow had never lacked. No one ever believed them when they said that his parents had named him Snow.

They had, but not in English.

"You know what I mean." Snow leaned back again, arranging himself against his black pillows. "She is not Anya."

Didn't he know it? S

era tied him in more knots than Anya had ever managed.

He wasn't sure whether he was coming or going where she was concerned.

When he was with her, everything felt right and good, incredible, and he could even go as far as to say that he was happy for the first time in many long years. He had never felt so alive, so content, as he did when he was in her arms, and he had never felt so connected to anyone.

When he was away from her though, the doubts began to creep in, the voices of his past whispering dark things to him, warnings about what could happen if he accepted Sera into his life and his heart.

"Do you think she loves you?" Snow said and Antoine frowned.

"I am not sure... not yet... I don't think so. Maybe she would in time."

Snow sighed again. "Good... I want you to have another chance at love. One of us deserves something good in our lives, and out of both of us, it should be you. You deserve it."

Antoine hated the note of resignation that lined the edge of his brother's voice. He was thinking about his death again, always seeking the easy way out. Antoine wouldn't let that happen. He would help him defeat his bloodlust and would see him happy before he did anything about pursuing his own happiness.

He touched his brother's hand and Snow met his gaze. "We both deserve someone who will love us for who we are and will not leave us, but it is not something I am looking for at this moment. I will not let anything stand between us, do you understand?"

Snow laughed mirthlessly. "I understand. You intend to make me keep that wretched promise. I grow tired of this hollow life, Brother... one day you will have to let me go."

Antoine squeezed his hand, his throat constricting even as anger seeped into his veins. "Never. Do you hear me, Snow? I will never let you go. I will help you defeat your bloodlust or I will die trying with you."

Snow closed his eyes and frowned. "I do not deserve such a sacrifice. I have seen the way you watch Javier with Lilah, and even Callum when he speaks with Kristina on his phone. I know you long for something good, warm and female in your life. Sera can be that woman for you. She can help heal your past and give you a future."

"Without you... that's what you are saying, is it not?" Antoine snapped and Snow's frown hardened. Antoine grabbed his brother's shoulders and shook him, intent on forcing him to open his eyes and look at him. He wanted to see the answer in his brother's eyes. They opened and met his, the terrible longing for death shining in them. "I will not let that happen, so get it out of your damn stubborn mind!"

Snow smiled, a bare tilting of the corners of his lips. "A man can hope. It has been centuries, Antoine, and I am not getting better."

"You are. You say I am too lost in my own pity to see when I am on to a good thing, that I want to cast aside all hope of finding someone who truly loves me and who will remain at my side forever... you are lost too, Brother. You are so convinced that your bloodlust is unbeatable that you do not see the progress you have made." Antoine loosened his grip on Snow's shoulders and raised one hand to his cheek, keeping his brother's attention on him so he could see the honesty in his eyes as well as feel the truth in his blood. "You brought yourself back the other night. Lilah soothed you and you did not wish to hurt Sera. You care about them and that stopped you from hurting them. I had the same sort of experience. I bit Sera and I found I could control myself. I stopped myself because I care about her and I did not want to hurt her."

Snow's smile widened. "So you admit that you do care about her?"

Antoine sighed and nodded. He should have known Snow would be able to draw the truth out of him one way or another.

"I do. Deeply. But that only gives me more reason to keep my distance."

Snow's face fell and he shook his head. "No, it gives you reason to move closer to her, not further away. I do have more awareness and control in the presence of the females. You are right. I know what Lilah means to Javier, and what Sera means to you, and I have no desire to hurt those I love. Not again."

Antoine slid his hand to the nape of Snow's neck and firmly held it. "I know. It is the strength of your emotions that gives you some control over the bloodlust. In time, we will wean you off your blood addiction and you will be well again. We will find a way to satisfy it and keep it under control. You seem well tonight and I am glad."

"I fed on waking, the same smaller quantity that I have been taking for the past few days now, and it seems to be working. The bloodlust has deemed me worthy of some time as a sane person."

It was said so lightly but Antoine could sense his brother's pain and the underlying fear. He knew in his heart that Snow didn't want to die, just as he didn't want to live cooped up in his room, shut away from the world. He did such things because he was afraid that the darkness would seize him and he would end up hurting those he loved again.

Antoine couldn't imagine what his brother felt as he sat alone in his room, unable to be with those he cared about because he might lose control, living each night with the past hanging over his head.

"Antoine." There was a note of caution in Snow's tone that drew a frown from Antoine. Snow glanced away and sighed. "Sera is good for you. Never forget that."

He didn't intend to, but why was Snow so insistent on him remembering that Sera was worthy of his affection and devotion.

"Snow?" Antoine's frown intensified. "What aren't you telling me?"

Snow closed his eyes. "Anya came to the theatre."

Antoine sat bolt upright. "What? When?"

He blinked rapidly, unsure whether he truly wanted the answers to those questions. He hadn't seen Anya in centuries. He had forgotten so much about her. He couldn't recall the colour of her eyes, or her face, or the smell of her. His mind and his heart were full of Sera now.

Sera's beautiful smile as she made him laugh, her forest green eyes as they twinkled at him after they had made love, and the way her ash blonde hair smelt as he slept close to her, snuggled up against her back with his arms tightly wrapped around her.

Snow slowly opened his eyes and fixed him with a hard look. "Keep hold of those feelings, Antoine. Do not be deceived again. Sera is good for you. I can feel it in you. You are a different person now. You are happier than I have ever seen you."

"When, Snow?"

"She came to the performance that you missed to be with Sera. I am glad you were not there. Anya does not deserve to see you again... remember that. She is not worthy of you."

Antoine appreciated his brother's support but he was talking about Anya, the woman he had spent a century with, and had searched for after that.

After she had left him and filled his mind with a need to find her, a need that had made him blind to what Snow had been going through.

"I did not want to tell you," Snow said and Antoine nodded, understanding why his brother had wanted to keep this from him.

Snow liked Sera, and so did Antoine. All these years, he had thought that when he found Anya again, he would want to rush out and see her, would want to be with her regardless of what was happening in his life at the time.

He felt none of those desires as he sat beside his brother, trying to take in the fact that Anya was back.

Snow was right.

Sera was good for him, and she was better than Anya.

She was everything he needed now, and forever.

He was glad that Snow had gone against his instincts and told him that Anya was in the city. It unnerved Antoine that she was so nearby and that she had come to the theatre, but at least he could prepare himself in case she returned.

Did she know it was his theatre?

Anya had always moved in the highest circles of society. Everyone knew who the owners of Vampirerotique were. Was it just coincidence that she had attended a performance then or had she come looking for him?

Antoine didn't care either way.

It was too late for her to come crawling back to him. He had finally moved on and would allow nothing to jeopardise what he had with Sera. His feelings for her were so much deeper than his for Anya had ever been. If Sera left him, he wouldn't go searching for her.

He would die.

What if he saw Anya though?

He didn't feel a desire to rush out and find her, but what if she came to his theatre and approached him?

He felt sure that his feelings for her were long dead, but a fragment of his heart was still uncertain. He wasn't sure how he would react if he saw her again.

Part of Antoine needed to see Sera, wanted to touch her and kiss her and chase away his lingering doubts by losing himself in her, but he wouldn't leave his brother. Snow needed the company.

"You will listen to your heart, Brother?" Snow stared at him, pale icy eyes dark and intense, as though he wouldn't accept anything other than a positive answer to his question.

Antoine nodded. "I will. Come, let us speak about better things."

"You have met the new males?" Snow said and Antoine was thankful for the change of subject.

He nodded again and told his brother about the two new vampires they would welcome into their ranks tonight, and talked about life at the theatre and how crazy the females had made the place. Positive things that chased the darkness from Snow's mind and gave him peace, and erased the shadow of Anya from his own mind.

He lost track of time as they talked and he endured Snow's lectures about Sera and not running from his feelings, not flinching when Snow cut close to the bone with his comments and observations, and his pressing him to remain with her and give her a chance.

When he glanced at the small digital clock on Snow's bedside table, it was close to midnight.

"Will you attend tonight?" Antoine said, hopeful that his brother would come down from his room to socialise with the others. Snow needed more than just his company. He needed to see with his own eyes that he could function in society still and that he didn't need to fear that his bloodlust would slip its tethers and place everyone in danger. "I am sure that everyone would like to see you, and you can continue lecturing me, or perhaps Sera. She would probably enjoy hearing all of my sordid secrets."

Snow grinned to reveal slightly extended canines, his pale eyes lighting up at the prospect of embarrassing him. "I could tell her that you wet the bed until you were in your thirties."

Antoine frowned. "We both know that thirty for a pureblood is like a human toddler. You would be giving her misinformation."

"It would still be funny to see her face." Snow shrugged his broad shoulders, his grin holding. He picked up his book from the bedside table and waved towards the door. "Go, spend some time with your female and leave me to my book."

Antoine rose, settled one knee on the bed and cupped the nape of his brother's neck. He leaned over Snow and pressed a kiss to his forehead.

"Get some rest and think about coming down to the party when it starts. Even a short time would be good for you." He rested his forehead against Snow's. "I will find a way to bring you peace, Brother, so hold on. Promise me you will hold on. I cannot lose you."

Snow wrapped one strong arm around him, cradling the back of his head, and pressed their foreheads harder together.

"You drive a hard bargain, Antoine. I will not give in because I know it would hurt you. I will keep fighting it. I promise."

Antoine placed another brief kiss on his brother's forehead and then released him and turned away in one swift movement so Snow didn't see the tears in his eyes. He cursed them and scrubbed them away with the heel of his right hand as he headed for the door.

He wouldn't fail his brother.

There was a way to defeat bloodlust and he would find it before it was too late and he lost the person he loved the most in his dark world.

He closed the door behind him and crossed the hall to his own door. He paused with his hand on the brass knob and leaned against the doorframe, battling his emotions as they threatened to overwhelm him. He wouldn't lose his brother. He had sworn to do all in his power to save him and he would.

The door opened and Sera was there, her eyebrows furrowed and concern shining in her beautiful green eyes.

She raised her arms, opening them to him, and he bit his lower lip, fighting back the tears. He stepped into her arms and gave up his own fight.

Sera wrapped him in her soft embrace, pressing kisses to his cheek and neck, whispering comforting words as he nestled his face against the crook of her neck.

Snow was right.

Sera wasn't something he should be turning his back on. She was something beautiful, magical, more wonderful than Anya had ever been, and he should be holding her closer, letting her into his heart. She gave him happiness and laughter. She gave him peace and love. She was his light that chased away the darkness.

He couldn't let her go.

Not now. Not ever.

She had changed him and he would never be the same. She had breathed life back into him and given him hope that a future with her would be one free of bloodlust, full of happiness and love.

He would never walk away from her.

He prayed she would never walk away from him.

CHAPTER 14

Sera felt more than a little self-conscious in the black cocktail dress that she had borrowed from Lilah. The slender brunette stood beside her, chatting animatedly to her lover, Javier, who was apparently her sire too.

Lilah had told her the whole amazing story behind their coming together while they had been getting ready in her apartment.

Sera had to admit that she was new enough to the vampire world that she hadn't heard about owned humans. She was glad that Elizabeth had chosen to bring her into her world as a vampire rather than a human slave though.

Javier had been charming during the brief moments he had appeared at the apartment, making sure she felt comfortable being in his and Lilah's home and wanted for nothing. Their apartment was a contrast to Antoine and Snow's. Javier's was shades of blue and paler tones, brighter and less dreary than the colours the two aristocrat vampires had chosen for their own apartments.

She had even met Javier's younger brother, Andreu, although he hadn't stayed long. He had been eager to head down to the party they were holding to welcome him and another elite vampire called Payne.

When Antoine had returned from his brother's room and come to her, her heart had ached for him. There had been so much pain in his blood and his eyes. He had been so desperate to kiss her and hold her, and she had given in to him, knowing that he needed comfort and wanting to give it to him any way that she could.

Antoine had told her that she looked beautiful when he had pulled away from her long enough to see her completed transformation. His gaze had lingered on the long elegant black dress, specifically the plunging neckline that revealed his marks on her throat and cleavage that she had needed a little help to attain.

Lilah didn't have a problem filling out her own deep emerald dress. The woman was blessed and a few of the men in the large brightly lit room had noticed, although all of them had looked away when threatened with a growl by Javier.

Sera tried to focus on the conversation but she couldn't get her mind off Antoine or what had happened in his apartment just minutes before they had come down to the party. She blushed each time she replayed it in her head. He had been rough with her, as though he couldn't control himself and his need for her. He had torn away her panties, lifted her and pinned her against the wall, taking her hard and fast, kissing her until she had felt dizzy and lost.

What had awoken such a primal need for a connection in him?

She knew in her heart that he had been seeking comfort, relief from whatever dark thoughts were plaguing him. She had enjoyed their wild moment, had experienced the most incredible orgasm, and the fierce way that Antoine had sunk his fangs into her throat and climaxed had left her feeling as though he had been staking a claim on her. She couldn't shake the questions filling her mind though.

What had driven Antoine to such desperation?

He had mentioned his brother but something in his eyes and their joined blood said it was more than that. There was something he wasn't telling her.

Payne muttered about blood under his breath as he stalked past, his dark air that of a man on a mission.

Javier had introduced her to the handsome blond elite and he hadn't said much other than a handful of rehearsed pleasantries. The moment the conversation had ebbed, he had made his excuses and left. She hadn't seen him speak to anyone other than Callum after that.

Whenever she caught sight of him, he was alone.

Callum had made his excuses too and Lilah had positively bubbled with excitement for him and Kristina, pressing him to relay her happiness for them to the female werewolf.

Sera ducked closer to Lilah when Victor glanced her way. She didn't want him to see her. He went back to speaking to a group of women, his grin wide as he towered over them, muscles stretching the suit he wore. He must have purchased a size too small because he looked as though he was about to tear the material when he moved to sling his arm around one of the women. She erupted into a giggling fit. Sera rolled her eyes and moved on, her thoughts stuck on the word Payne had grumbled.

Blood.

She was parched.

A quick scan of the busy room didn't reveal any sign of someone handing out blood. No one was holding glasses either.

What sort of vampire party happened without some refreshments on offer?

Maybe they would come later. She pushed away her hunger and looked for Antoine instead.

After he had led her down the stairs with her arm looped around his and his hand holding hers against his forearm, and had introduced her to a few people so she felt comfortable, he had begun to circulate.

At the time, she'd had no interest in tottering around the room on the heels Lilah had lent her so she had remained with the pretty young vampire and her doting mate.

Now she wished she had gone with him.

She hadn't expected him to be away from her for so long and she wanted to know that he was okay.

Her gaze caught on someone as they entered and she smiled.

Snow strolled across the room, his movements casual even though he radiated caution that caused everyone in his path to move out of his way. His mouth quirked into a smile when he spotted her and he changed course, heading towards her and the others where they stood near one of the black walls.

He was taller than she remembered when he came to a halt beside her, his immense frame overshadowing her. Even Javier and Andreu looked small compared with him.

Sera's smile widened. "You know, I think this is the first time I've seen you fully dressed."

She raked her gaze over him, taking in the crisp black trousers and the gunmetal grey shirt he had paired with them. The clothes were tailored for him, fitting his broad body perfectly and accentuating his build with devastating effect. A few of the females passing by glanced his way, eyes showing a flicker of interest as well as fear.

Sera felt it too.

Snow was handsome in a feral sort of way, a man who radiated danger at a strength that would turn most women away from him. It would take a strong woman to seize this man's heart and keep hold of it.

Lilah giggled, her golden eyes bright with it. "I think it's a first for me too."

Javier growled and his grip on Lilah's waist tightened, drawing her into his body. Sera smiled at how protective he was of his mate, and jealous too.

"You look good," she said to Snow and he shrugged, clearly uncomfortable with her praising him.

"You should look in the mirror," he said, voice low and rough, almost a growl of appreciation. "Has my brother seen you in that dress?"

She nodded and twirled for him, blushing from the memories of her heated moment with Antoine in his room and the feel of Snow's gaze on her. "He has."

"And he still managed to drag himself away to play the host?" Snow grinned and shook his head. "My brother needs to reassess his priorities. If you were my female, I would not let you out of my reach... like Javier with Lilah."

Javier frowned and loosened his grip a little. "You are in a good mood tonight, Snow."

Snow's pale eyebrows rose. "I am. I feel good."

Sera listened to their banter, feeling strange as she watched them laugh and tease each other. She felt as though she had fallen into their group and they had accepted her with open arms, welcoming her into a theatre that felt more like a family than a business.

As Snow talked, a hint of red touched his irises and then faded again.

How in control of himself was he?

The crimson that bloomed in his icy eyes at times scared her but she felt sorry for him too. If Antoine was right and Snow couldn't remember the terrible things he had done, she pitied him all the more. She could understand why Antoine refused to tell him though. He wanted to protect Snow, and everyone he cared about.

The smell of blood drifted past her and she turned, thinking someone had finally opened the bar. Her gaze fell on a beautiful woman drenched in scarlet, bleeding profusely from long gashes on her arms and clutching her stomach. She walked forwards, stumbling towards the centre of the room. Vampires all around her backed away. One stood his ground.

Antoine.

A flood of panic surged through Sera. The woman was going to hurt him.

She rushed two steps towards him and then her feet froze, her heart turning to ice in her chest. Antoine's usually cold eyes were warm as he approached the woman, full of disbelief that she could feel in her blood through their lingering connection.

Disbelief that was rapidly becoming panic and concern.

Sera looked back over her shoulder at Snow to gauge his reaction to the woman and the look he gave her said it all. His surprise quickly became pity. The red around his irises increased as the scent of blood grew stronger.

Sera wasn't sure how to react as she turned back to watch Antoine with the woman. Her blood carried the scent of fear and Sera wasn't sure whether she would last much longer without assistance.

Her heart ached.

She had never wanted anyone dead, but she wished for it now.

"Antoine... help me," the woman said and reached for him, her steps faltering. "I am sorry for all I did... I was scared... but I always... followed your life. I came here... to see you. Please, Antoine... help me."

She collapsed and Antoine caught her, going down with her and breaking her fall. He knelt on the wooden floor with her in his arms, his face a mask of horror, pale eyes wide and blood relaying feelings to Sera that cleaved her heart open.

"Hold on," he whispered and scooped her up into his arms, rising with her. "I need to get you out of here."

The look of concern that filled his eyes slashed at Sera, cutting another deep wound in her heart.

She felt ill as she watched him carry the woman out of the room, adrift and lost, her legs trembling and heart threatening to shatter. Part of her said to leave now before anyone could say anything to her. She didn't want to hear their questions or see the pity in Snow's eyes.

Antoine loved this woman.

He wanted to be with this woman and she should let him be with her, not stand between them.

She had realised shortly after finally meeting Antoine that he would never love her as he loved the woman who had been in his heart for centuries.

Sera turned to make her excuses and leave, but Snow's hand on her arm stopped her. She looked up into his eyes and saw more red in them. His hand shook against her.

"Are you unwell?" She grabbed both of his arms to steady him when he swayed.

Snow gritted his teeth. "Can you lend me a hand?"

Sera nodded without thinking, her mind wholly on helping him because she could see that he was fighting hard against whatever darkness was trying to seize control and there was so much pain and fear in his eyes.

She cared about him, had grown to like him in the short space of time they had spent together, and she wouldn't leave him in his hour of need.

She manoeuvred his arm around her shoulders, unafraid of how it placed her close to him, her belief that he wouldn't hurt her as strong as the one she had about Antoine. She helped him from the room.

The scent of blood lingered in the staircase that led up to the floor where his apartment and the others were, and didn't lessen until she had passed Antoine's door. Antoine must have taken his woman to his apartment to help her. Sera ignored her anger and jealousy and kept walking, focusing all of her attention on Snow.

He needed her and she wouldn't fail him.

He clumsily banged into the panelled door of his apartment and fumbled with the handle.

"Let me." Sera gently took his hand away, twisted the knob and pushed the door open for him.

He thanked her with a tight smile and she helped him inside, leading him over to the bed.

When they reached it, he collapsed onto the black covers and sprawled out, breathing hard.

Sera raced back to the door, closed and locked it.

As much as she feared being alone and trapped with Snow, she feared him escaping even more. Not for the sake of those on the other side of the door, but for his sake.

She didn't want him to suffer more than he already had. He feared being around people and was afraid that he would lose control and hurt them. It must have taken a lot of courage for him to come to the party tonight.

His breathing was too laboured for him to speak. He grunted and stretched one arm out.

Towards the restraints fixed to one of the thick metal bedposts.

Sera nodded.

She grunted herself when she tried to haul Snow up the bed. Dear God, he weighed a tonne. Sera kicked off her heels, mounted the bed and stood near his shoulders. She hooked her hands under his armpits and dragged him, growling with effort. Her bottom banged into the wall behind his headboard and she looked down at Snow. He was already fumbling with one restraint, trying to close it around his right wrist.

Sera gingerly moved over him, trying not to draw too much attention to herself in case it prompted him to lose control and tear her throat open.

She knelt on the bed, covered his left hand with hers and smiled when he looked at her, the red filling almost all of his irises now. She closed the cuff around his wrist and locked it, and Snow collapsed onto his back, breathing hard and radiating his struggle in waves so strong that she felt it right down in her core.

He was fighting it but he was losing.

She hitched her long black dress up and scrambled over him, risking his wrath. He surprised her by placing his other wrist in the open cuff on his bed. He was more coherent than she had thought. She locked the cuff around his wrist and moved to his feet.

She had to tug his boots off to get at his ankles and Snow growled when she was none too gentle about it. She smiled her apology at him and dragged each foot to the corners of his bed so the restraints reached them. When she had both ankles secured, Snow began to settle and his breathing became more controlled.

Sera backed towards the door. She had helped him and now she had to go, before anything else happened.

"Wait." Snow opened his eyes. His pupils were changing. He sucked in a hard breath and gritted his teeth, lips peeling back to reveal his huge fangs. "Do not leave. My brother... he is worth fighting for."

Sera stopped and took a step towards Snow. He wrestled the restraints, growling at them, and then settled again.

"He makes mistakes... does not say or do the right thing at times... but he is worthy of being loved." Snow struggled to sit up and failed, the restraints stretching his arms too tightly for him to get any leverage from his elbows. Sera moved closer to him so he could see her. His eyes were completely red now, his pupils stretched into narrowed slits. "He deserves to be loved... after all I have put him through."

He looked so sad that Sera couldn't stop herself from sitting on the bed beside him.

"I have put him through so much." Tears lined his eyes and Sera resisted the urge to lay her hand on his cheek to comfort him. "It haunts me."

"I know," she whispered and laid her hand on his chest.

His heart pounded like a drum against her palm through his dark shirt, strong and powerful.

"If I could make his life better, I would do whatever it took... if you have feelings for him... then fight for him." Snow closed his eyes and frowned, tipping his head back into the black pillows. Tears cut down his temples and soaked into his white hair. He snarled, his body as taut as a bowstring, and then relaxed into the bed again. He panted and looked at her, his pupils struggling between cat-like slits and circles. "Do not let Antoine draw away from you just because of the terrible acts I committed."

An icy chill washed through her. Snow knew. Good Lord. He knew what he had done, not just to Antoine, but to his whole family.

Sera couldn't stop herself then. She cupped his cheek, hoping to comfort him.

"He needs you. He just does not realise how much. Make him see. Sera. You are right for him. Not her. Never her."

Sera nodded and held his cheek. She didn't want to talk about that right now. She wanted to talk to him, to make him tell her that he knew what he had done. She felt sure that part of the reason his bloodlust had such a firm grip on him was those memories.

He needed to share the burden with someone in order to overcome it, just as Antoine had confided everything in her, but that someone wasn't her and it wasn't Antoine. Snow clearly didn't want Antoine to know and she could understand that. Antoine already suffered enough as it was.

That was why part of her wanted to leave.

"I want Antoine to be happy, Snow, with all of my heart... and he will be now that she has come back to him."

Snow shook his head. "You are wrong. I have seen him with her and I have seen him with you... Sera... and it is you who will make him happiest. Do not give up on him."

Could he be right?

It was too much to hope that he was, even when it was what she truly wanted. She wanted Antoine to be happy and with her. She didn't want to lose him.

She had already fought so hard for him.

Sera frowned.

She had.

She had fought for him and had come too far to give up now.

The doorknob rattled, a harsh curse sounded on the other side, and then there was a scrape of metal on metal.

Sera turned to look over her shoulder at the door just as it opened, revealing a bloodied and panic-stricken Antoine. She didn't take her hand away from Snow's cheek. Her heart thundered, adrenaline flooding her veins and making her tremble as she waited for Antoine to speak, afraid that he would say how happy he was now that Anya had returned and that he wanted her to leave.

Antoine fixed wild eyes on them. "I didn't know what to expect when Javier told me you had left with Snow."

Antoine looked relieved when he saw his brother restrained and then his eyes darkened when they stopped on her hand where it rested against Snow's face.

He growled.

Snow raised a single pale eyebrow at his brother. "Thank you for your low opinion of me. I can control myself around a beautiful woman."

Antoine's eyes flashed red and he snarled.

Was Snow trying to piss him off?

Her eyes widened.

No.

He was trying to prove to her that his brother cared more for her than he did for Anya.

Antoine stalked over to her and yanked her hand away from his brother's face, holding her wrist in a bruising grasp. "And what did you think you were doing leaving with Snow?"

Sera frowned up at him.

She wasn't about to sit down and take that sort of attitude from him.

He might be around a thousand years her senior and an aristocrat, but she wasn't some serving wench he could order around and treat like his subordinate.

She rose to her feet, squaring up to him, forcing him to back off a step, and tore his hand from her arm.

"Snow wanted my assistance and I could judge what he needed me for, so I came with him to help him restrain himself. It was the least I could do before I left."

"Left?" Antoine's anger melted as his eyes widened and then they narrowed on her, red bleeding into them. "Why are you leaving?"

"She isn't," Snow piped up and Antoine's gaze flickered to him at the same time as hers did.

"I'm not. I am. I don't know. I'm not?" she asked Snow and he shook his head.

"You're not."

Sera dragged in a deep breath and sharply exhaled it. Having an immense, dangerous vampire, a man who was the older brother of the one she wanted, on her side was certainly good for her courage. She felt brave knowing that Snow had her back. She couldn't fail. She straightened and faced Antoine again.

She wouldn't fail.

"I'm not leaving. She is."

"She?" Antoine looked lost.

Snow huffed. "Anya."

"Anya," Antoine echoed.

"The woman you left the party with? I know you still have feelings for her... love that has lasted centuries. I get that. I saw the look in your eyes when she fell into your arms tonight... but I'm not going to stand by and let her just walk back into your life and take you from me." Sera prodded her fingertip against Antoine's hard chest, digging it deeper with each word.

Her heart raced and blood rushed, knees weakening with each passing second. She wouldn't falter.

Snow was right.

If she wanted Antoine, she had to fight for him, and she would, even if it was a fight to the death with the bitch who had broken his heart.

"Look?" Antoine frowned, his frustration flowing through her blood, and glanced over at Snow. "Are you alright? I did my best to get her out of the room straight away. I should not have brought her up here. My office might have been the better choice. I wasn't thinking."

It dawned on Sera that the look of concern in Antoine's eyes when he had seen Anya bloodied and injured hadn't been for her. She slowly turned her head towards Snow and looked at him, eyes wide and her body numb as she realised the gravity of her mistake.

Antoine had been concerned about Snow.

He had known the smell of blood would trigger Snow's hunger and had tried to stop that from happening by quickly removing the source of the scent. That was also the reason why there hadn't been blood on offer at the party. Antoine had wanted Snow to come down and socialise, and had taken steps to make sure his brother would be comfortable.

Sera felt so stupid.

She had mistaken Antoine's concern as love for the woman when it had been love for his brother.

"I am fine, thanks to Sera." Snow looked at her and smiled softly, his eyes barely touched with crimson now. "Remember what I said."

Sera nodded and felt a little more confident as Antoine turned back to her. He smiled warmly, his blue eyes bright with it, and placed his hands on her hips and drew her up against his hard body. Sera refused to give in to him, even when his smile widened. Mercy, he knew how to melt a woman's heart.

"You were saying something about not letting someone take me from you?" he said and she blushed. He swept his fingers over the marks on her throat.

Sera dropped her chin but Antoine didn't let her escape. He placed his fingers under her chin and raised it, forcing her eyes back to his. They were so warm now, a sea of feelings that she would willingly drown in. She could die happy lost in this man's eyes, or in his arms.

"I won't let her take you from me, Antoine. I fought too damn hard for you to lose you now, or ever. As soon as she's able to move, she is out of here. I mean it. I want her gone. No one in this world is going to come between us." Sera glanced over her shoulder at Snow. "Present company excluded."

Snow just smiled.

Sera turned back to Antoine, her jaw set and heart steady. Snow had told her to make Antoine see that she was the one for him, the only one out of her and Anya who could make him happy.

She wasn't normally the type to command people, but then she hadn't been the type to seduce someone either before she had found herself falling for Antoine.

For him, she would do anything, no matter how embarrassing it was.

If it would make him see that what they had together was stronger than what he'd had with Anya and that she intended to keep fighting for him, because she was falling for him and she needed him more than anything, and that she would love him forever and never hurt him, then she would lay it all on the line right here and right now.

"I refuse to let you go and I'm sure as hell not about to let you or anyone else make me leave. You are mine, Antoine." She snaked her arms around Antoine's neck and drew him down for a slow, unhurried kiss.

Antoine's hands settled against her lower back, holding her close to him as he kissed her, so softly and lightly that she felt as though she was floating. He pressed a final brief kiss to her lips and then pulled back to look down into her eyes.

"And you are mine." His blue eyes shone with the promise behind those words, one of love and forever. His breathtaking smile warmed her right down to her soul. There was so much affection and happiness in that smile. Happiness that she had given him. "Anya got herself into a fight with a werewolf pack, but her injuries will not take long to heal. I will move her into one of the dormitory rooms and she will be gone soon. I would never allow her to come between us, Sera. I need you and you mean too much to me. If you wish her gone sooner, I will arrange for a doctor to take her away this night."

The woman had been bleeding profusely from multiple lacerations. She didn't look as though she was in any state to be moved tonight and Sera would never let her jealousy control her enough that she placed someone's life at risk, but she appreciated the gesture.

"Move her out of the apartment and she can stay until she's fit to leave, but I don't want you near her."

Antoine's smile widened, as though he liked the jealous hiss that had been in her words and the possessive way she held onto him.

"As my lady desires." He touched the marks on her throat again.

"They do suit her," Snow said. "I take it she was yours long before tonight?"

Sera frowned at him. "Whatever do you mean?"

Antoine dropped a kiss on the scars and she looked back at him, deep into his eyes. There was an edge of concern in them now.

"Yes, Antoine, whatever do I mean?" Snow's voice rang with amusement.

Antoine scowled at him and then smiled at her. His thumb swept over the marks.

"You are young, so you probably do not know, but in the time I was born and raised, biting another vampire was a show of possession." He continued to stroke the place where he had bitten her. "I still believe in the old ways... so when I say that you are mine, Sera, I mean that you are mine, irrevocably, eternally."

Antoine pulled her back to him and covered her mouth with his, stealing her voice with a kiss that had her leaning into him for more, uncaring of their company. She smiled against his lips, warm from head to toe, victorious.

She had risked everything to pursue a man who others believed was emotionless and had discovered that he was warm, loving, and beautiful.

She had done all in her power to gain an audience so she could win his attention and had ended up wanting to win his heart and give him happiness.

She had been through so much with him already but she knew this was only the start, that the years ahead would both test and reward them, and she was determined to see it through and remain at Antoine's side.

He had placed a claim on her.

She was his now.

And he was hers.

Irrevocably.

Eternally.

The End

Read on for a preview of the next book in the London Vampires romance series, Enslave!

ENSLAVE

Andreu watched the show unfolding.

Tonight's opening performance of the winter season was in full swing and to a packed house. It seemed that many of the aristocrat and elite vampires that had refused to set foot in Vampirerotique after discovering that one of the owners had fallen for and impregnated a werewolf had come crawling back, unable to find another theatre that could provide the erotic bloody fix they needed to satisfy their darker hungers.

That was the sort of addiction that Andreu wanted for the theatre he planned to open.

Filling in for his older brother, Javier, at Vampirerotique was nothing more than temporary, half a year in which he would learn all that he could from the place and build some connections for himself. He had no interest in emulating Javier by becoming a slave to a business and binding himself to a single female.

A century ago, when Javier had first told him that he was leaving Spain to open an erotic theatre in London that catered to their kind and provided live human performers, Andreu had been all for it. It had sounded like a fantastic business. It was, but Javier's approach to the business left a lot to be desired in Andreu's eyes.

When he opened his own theatre in the busy city of Barcelona, he wasn't going to help run the damn thing. He would hire capable elite vampires to do the day-to-day work for him and would oversee it all from a distance, and reap the rewards.

Enough money to keep him set for life and a reputation that would get him into even the most exclusive vampire clubs and would bring him a flock of females to satisfy his every carnal need.

Life would be good.

Pleasure and fun. That was what he wanted and the quickest way to get it was to get famous, get rich, and stay single.

Javier had it all wrong. Andreu couldn't imagine what had possessed him to do something as foolish as chaining himself not only to his business but also to one woman for the rest of his long life.

Andreu leaned back in his crimson velvet seat, kicked his feet up to rest on the low curved wall that enclosed the private box, and clasped his hands behind his head, the motion causing his black designer suit jacket to fall open and reveal his equally dark shirt.

He smiled and surveyed the eager audience stretched out below him and then those in the boxes that lined the wall opposite him, all of their eyes glued to the two male humans and the female vampire on the stage.

Life would be very good indeed.

The huge black four-poster bed in the middle of the stage was a new set piece. The human male chained to it by his ankles and wrists was a new twist too.

Antoine, the aristocrat who handled most of the business, had decided to mix things up a little now that they were in the winter season and the night hours were longer, giving them more time for the performances. There had been many changes in the past five weeks, and not only in the shows.

He had respected Antoine once. The man had a head for business and a reputation for having a detached attitude that had given Andreu the impression that he was only interested in profit and pleasure, but it turned out that Andreu had been wrong.

The pretty female blonde vampire wrapped tightly in Antoine's arms where the powerful aristocrat stood in his usual position to the side of the audience in the stalls, watching the show, had been the first indication that Antoine wasn't his sort of man after all. The female of their species had lured him into submission too, and that was just the tip of the iceberg.

What lurked beneath the water was Snow.

Andreu didn't intend to show it, but Snow scared the hell out of him.

The huge male with platinum hair and eyes like ice was frightening enough on a good night.

When he had a bad one, the man was dangerous.

Insane.

What had possessed Javier to ask the two aristocrats for help when he and Callum had been setting up the theatre?

There were a thousand better choices in aristocrat society than these brothers. Bloodlust gripped Snow most nights, and probably infected Antoine too. If both of them lost control, it would be a bloodbath.

Andreu shuddered at the thought.

No way in Hell would he be sticking around if that happened. It was every vampire for himself in that sort of situation and Andreu would be first out of the door.

The woman in Antoine's arms, Sera, turned and looked up at her lover. Antoine dipped his head, as though pressing a kiss to her cheek, and she went back to watching the show.

Sera had been on edge until only recently, annoyed by the presence of an injured woman who had once been Antoine's lover. The aristocrat female's wounds had healed and she had been gone for a few days now, long enough that Sera looked more relaxed around her man.

She smiled more now and had spoken to Andreu several times, although he hadn't really made much effort to converse with her. He had spent the past few weeks learning the ropes from Javier. His work seemed easy enough, and it had its perks.

The female vampire on stage, a pretty petite redhead dressed in a black leather thong, thigh-high boots and a matching black studded bra, chained the second nude human male's wrists above his head, attaching them to the top of one of the bedposts. She kissed him until he strained for more and then backed away.

Andreu quirked a dark eyebrow as she unhooked a whip from her side and the human male turned around. She cracked the whip across his back, leaving a red streak, and the scent of blood drifted up to Andreu.

The man was strong. Whoever had selected him had known he had potent blood that would get the audience leaning forwards and eager for more. Andreu didn't want to fall for the same lure as everyone else in the theatre, but he found himself dropping his feet to the floor and sitting up.

Javier remained relaxed beside him.

Andreu cursed his older brother for having stronger self-control and settled back into his seat, watching the woman as she struck the man again. He cried out this time and a ripple of pleasure flowed through the theatre in response, murmurs of excitement following in its wake. Nothing got a vampire's blood pumping like the scent of blood laced with fear and pain.

The naked dark-haired male on the bed writhed with each strike she placed on the other man, his hips grinding and bucking. Low moans escaped him as he tilted his head back into the pillows. Andreu's brow quirked again.

The female vampire was transferring her own pleasure to the male, her own desire and arousal, keeping him subdued but hungry for more. The man chained to the bedpost turned around to face his dark mistress, his eyes screwed shut in evident pain. She didn't stop. She cracked the whip across his chest, leaving a long red gash that dripped blood down flexed stomach muscles.

Andreu sucked in a sharp breath as she rewarded the human male, licking the rivulets of crimson from his chest and then stroking her tongue along the line where the whip had struck him. Devil. He wanted a show like this in his own theatre.

He leaned forwards, resting one arm on the low carved wall of the box, his gaze glued to the woman as she writhed against the man, tasting blood that Andreu wanted on his own tongue.

He breathed deeply to steady himself as his fangs emerged, pressing against his lips.

He definitely wanted a show like this one on his own stage. He had been to plenty of erotic vampire shows in his years, especially the past century, but he had never witnessed one that had such darkness and such deviation.

The petite redhead unchained the man and wrapped slender fingers around his steel collar.

She lured him to the bed with her and left him at the foot of the mattress, near the other man's feet.

Andreu frowned, nostrils flaring and blood on the verge of heating with desire as she crawled up the length of the man chained to the bed. He strained to reach her, unable to move his hands more than an inch in his cuffs.

The female removed her underwear, teased her breasts and the man at the same time, and then settled herself onto his cock.

The man bucked up, hissing and grunting, tugging on his restraints as the woman rode him with a few swift, brutal thrusts, and then stopped. He begged for more.

Was she lessening her control over him? Normally human thralls didn't speak. They felt only what their master fed to them. In the case of erotic shows, they felt pleasure, bliss, and ecstasy. Everything the vampire controlling them experienced.

The huge screen that hung at the back of the stage projected everything she did with her two male thralls. She looked over her shoulder at the other man, coy and innocent, her youthful face flushed with heat and dark eyes wide. A siren. What man would be able to resist such a pure-looking woman?

The man behind her stroked his erection and then came to her, obeying her silent command. He pushed her forwards with force that confirmed to Andreu that she had indeed lessened her control over the two men and was going to let them have their way for a while before she ended the show by feeding from them. She moaned loudly as he parted her buttocks and filled her with his rigid cock.

Andreu glanced at Javier. His brother wasn't watching the show. He was on his mobile phone. Andreu shook his head and leaned back so he could catch a glimpse of the screen. A picture of Lilah filled a square to the side of the message he was reading. Andreu sighed.

"I thought this was supposed to be a brotherly bonding session?" Andreu said, his English thick with his Spanish accent.

Javier looked up, the phone screen illuminating his face, and smiled.

Sickening.

The glow in his brown eyes had Andreu close to giving up on this whole night and telling his brother to get the hell out of his sight and back to his woman.

Love.

It had turned their sister into some heartsick girl when she had once been a hardheaded businesswoman. Now it had crippled his brother.

Dios, if it came for him next he would run as fast as he could.

It was bad enough that their parents, his mother in particular, had already begun with the whole 'one marriage leads to another' drivel just because their sister had married and then Javier had almost got himself killed in pursuit of Lilah, and now they were marrying.

"She is looking at dresses with Kristina and has seen one that she likes, but believes it is too expensive." Javier's dark eyes twinkled with affection.

"How much?" Andreu played along, only because his brother would want to talk about it and it was quicker and less painful to let him get it out and then they could get on with their evening. He intended to take his brother out to some London clubs, get him drunk on blood, and then lecture him about the perils of marriage and sacrificing bachelorhood for a woman.

"Five thousand."

"Pounds?" Andreu almost choked. "On a dress... for one day?"

Javier shrugged, his shoulders lifting his dark suit jacket, and began typing, thumbs moving fast over the on-screen keyboard, his sickening smile still in place. "Whatever my love wants, my love will have."

Andreu blew out a sigh and went to look back at the stage.

The hairs on the back of his neck prickled.

His senses spiked.

Someone was watching him. Andreu frowned. No. Not him. Javier had stiffened too, his fingers paused against the phone, and Andreu could feel him scouring the area with his senses. Andreu looked around at the other boxes and noticed that other vampires were suddenly on edge too.

Antoine had wrapped one arm across his woman's chest, his hand clutching her upper arm as his pale blue eyes scanned the theatre. The side doors close to them burst open, causing some of the audience to jump, and the white-haired demon that was Snow strode up to Antoine.

"Something isn't right," Javier said beside Andreu and he nodded in agreement. Something was very wrong.

The performance continued unaffected. Less than a quarter of the audience showed signs of tension. Was it only vampires over a certain age that could sense whatever presence had just entered the theatre?

Andreu scoured the three tiers of private boxes across the theatre from him, trying to find what they had all sensed. Nothing out of the ordinary in any of them but the feeling in the pit of his stomach wasn't going anywhere.

The moans and deep groans from the stage distracted him and made it hard to focus but he kept searching, unwilling to let his guard down when someone powerful and non-vampire was so close to him.

Javier finished his message, stood and slipped his phone into the pocket of his tailored black trousers. "I'm going down to speak with Antoine and Snow."

Andreu nodded. "I'll keep looking from up here. Be careful."

Javier's expression was grim as he nodded and placed his hand on Andreu's shoulder, squeezing it through his black suit jacket. "You too."

Perhaps taking his brother out for a much-needed night on the town would have to wait. Whatever had just entered the theatre showed no sign of leaving and they needed to know what they were dealing with, just in case it turned out to be something dangerous. Vampires were powerful, stronger than most creatures, but there were some out there that made his species look as frail as human babies.

Andreu stood and clutched the carved edge of the private box. He scanned the crowd below him, catching his brother crossing the strip of red carpet between the front row of seats and the black stage out of the corner of his eye. His senses touched on everyone and each came back as a vampire. Where was their uninvited guest?

He leaned forwards, trying to see all the boxes on his side of the theatre. He couldn't see into any of them.

Andreu looked down at Javier as he joined Antoine and the female vampire still held protectively in his arms. Snow was gone. Andreu found him closer to the back of the theatre, staring across at the boxes around Andreu.

Looking for their intruder.

If they were on Andreu's side of the theatre, Snow would find them. Andreu focused on scanning the boxes opposite him again, one by one this time, studying each of the occupants. Every single one of them was a vampire.

Was it possible they were mistaken?

The feeling at the nape of his neck and deep in his gut said it wasn't. Someone was here, something dark and powerful, and dangerous.

Andreu went to look down at his brother. His gaze froze on a beautiful woman with jagged jaw-length dark hair and a strapless bodice, short skirt and over-knee stockings combo that set his blood pounding.

There was something unusual about her and it wasn't just the fact that she was perched on the wall of an otherwise empty private box at the front of the middle tier, nearest the stage, one hand on it between her booted feet to hold her steady.

She seemed engrossed but as he stared at her, she slowly turned her head and her eyes met his across the theatre.

The whole world shrank between them until he swore he could see the incredible colours of her eyes and a million volts ran through him, setting every nerve ending alight. His heart exploded into action and his blood boiled like liquid fire in his veins.

"Dios," Andreu breathed, lost in a haze that came over him and veiled everything other than her. She was bright in the centre of so much darkness, a shining colourful light that drew him to her. A dazzling jewel like no other. A jewel he wanted to possess. He placed one foot up on the low wall surrounding his box, intent on crossing the theatre to her.

She disappeared.

The theatre popped back into existence and Andreu wobbled on the wall. His eyes shot down to the thirty-foot drop to the stalls below. He stumbled backwards and collapsed into the soft velvet seat behind him, breathing hard to settle the panic that had instantly chilled the heat in his blood.

"Cristo," Andreu whispered and stared wide-eyed across the theatre to the box where the woman had been.

And was now gone.

Disappeared.

He panted, his heart still thumping against his chest and shivers still skittering over his skin.

Whatever she was, she wasn't a vampire.

Whatever she was, he wanted her.

He would find her, and when he did, he would have her.

ENSLAVE

His determination to succeed in business has left no room in his life for love. Now, a beautiful and deadly succubus has teleported into his dark, decadent world and is in danger of enslaving his heart.

Andreu's future entails opening an erotic theatre like Vampirerotique, gaining wealth, women and power, not shackling himself to a single female, but he cannot deny the dangerously seductive succubus who stirs his anger and passion, and tempts him like no other—he will have her.

The moment their eyes meet, Varya knows she cannot have the exotic dark vampire who sets her pulse racing. His shadowed aura marks him as forbidden, but the hungers he awakens in her are too intense to resist—she must have a taste.

When an erotically-charged kiss ignites their soul-searing passion and reveals something dangerous about Andreu, will Varya leave forever or will she dare to risk all in pursuit of something she thought was beyond her reach?

Available now in ebook and paperback

ABOUT THE AUTHOR

Felicity Heaton is a New York Times and USA Today best-selling author who writes passionate paranormal romance books. In her books she creates detailed worlds, twisting plots, mind-blowing action, intense emotion and heart-stopping romances with leading men that vary from dark deadly vampires to sexy shape-shifters and wicked werewolves, to sinful angels and hot demons!

If you're a fan of paranormal romance authors Lara Adrian, J R Ward, Sherrilyn Kenyon, Gena Showalter, Larissa Ione and Christine Feehan then you will enjoy her books too.

If you love your angels a little dark and wicked, her best-selling Her Angel romance series is for you. If you like strong, powerful, and dark vampires then try the Vampires Realm romance series or any of her stand alone vampire romance books. If you're looking for vampire romances that are sinful, passionate and erotic then try her London Vampires romance series. Or if you like hot-blooded alpha heroes who will let nothing stand in the way of them claiming their destined woman then try her Eternal Mates series. It's packed with sexy heroes in a world populated by elves, vampires, fae, demons, shifters, and more. If sexy Greek gods with incredible powers battling to save our world and their home in the Underworld are more your thing, then be sure to step into the world of Guardians of Hades.

If you have enjoyed this story, please take a moment to contact the author at **author@felicityheaton.com** or to post a review of the book online

Connect with Felicity:
Website – http://www.felicityheaton.com
Blog – http://www.felicityheaton.com/blog/
Twitter – http://twitter.com/felicityheaton
Facebook – http://www.facebook.com/felicityheaton
Goodreads – http://www.goodreads.com/felicityheaton
Mailing List – http://www.felicityheaton.com/newsletter.php

FIND OUT MORE ABOUT HER BOOKS AT:
http://www.felicityheaton.com

Printed in Great Britain
by Amazon

67245519R00102